THE
HOCKEY MACHINE

THE HOCKEY MACHINE

MATT CHRISTOPHER

**Illustrated
by Richard Schroeppel**

Little, Brown and Company

BOSTON · NEW YORK · TORONTO · LONDON

First Paperback Edition

The characters and events in this book are fictitious. Any similarity to real persons, living or dead, is coincidental and not intended by the author.

Library of Congress Cataloging-in-Publication Data

Christopher, Matt.
    The hockey machine.
    Summary: Abducted by a "fan" and forced to become a member of a professional junior hockey team, thirteen-year-old star center Steve Crandall quickly realizes that he must play not only to win but to survive.
ISBN 0-316-14055-4 (hc)
ISBN 0-316-14087-2 (pb)
    [1. Hockey — Fiction.   2. Mystery and detective stories]
I. Schroeppel, Richard, ill.   II. Title.
PZ7.C458Ho   1986   [Fic]   86-10276

10 9

MV-NY

Published simultaneously in Canada
by Little, Brown & Company (Canada) Limited

Printed in the United States of America

to Duane and Karen

Chapter 1

The sharp, glistening ice skates almost slid out from under Steve Crandall as he banged into the boards flanking the curved sides of the rink. Keeping his balance, he caromed off the boards and sped after the loose puck.

He and the flashy Buckeye center, Jack Finlay, reached it at the same time. Realizing that Jack had a better chance of getting the puck than he, Steve rammed into him with a body check. A grunt tore from Jack as the blow sent him sprawling onto the ice.

Steve hooked the puck with his stick and carried it across the blue line into neutral territory. As two Buckeyes charged at him he passed the puck to right wingman Eddie Traynor.

Just then one of the Buckeyes' skates struck Steve's left skate, knocking him off balance. He fell and skidded on the ice in a slow spin. Disgusted, he scrambled to his feet, glanced around, and saw Eddie pass the puck to Stu Pierce, the Buckeyes' tall, speedy left wingman.

The pass was a poor one. The puck zipped behind Stu where he couldn't get it in spite of his quick, ice-flying stop. It ricocheted against the boards back into the face-off circle. A Buckeyes' defenseman intercepted it and slapped it toward the boards in an effort to put it back into Bobtails' territory.

But Steve could see a play in the making. He skated almost to the exact spot where he expected the puck to ricochet on the ice, hooked it with his stick

2

and dribbled it down alongside the rink. He hardly kept his eyes on it as he stickhandled it, moving the hard rubber disk forward with expert, back-and-forth movements.

He saw the Buckeyes' goalie crouched in the crease near the corner of the goal. A Buckeyes' defenseman stood at the goalie's left side, also waiting for an anticipated shot. So far, with the game in the middle of the third period, Steve had racked up five points out of the seven that the Bobtails had scored. What's wrong with shooting for a sixth? he thought.

The open space to the left of the goalie was Steve's target. It wasn't a big one, but he had scored in smaller ones.

Just as a Buckeyes' wingman charged at him, Steve slapped the puck with a hard, solid blow. The disk rose off the ice and flew toward the open space so fast only a few pairs of eyes were able to follow it. Both the defensive man and the goalie raised their gloved hands in

3

a desperate try to catch it, then dropped them helplessly as the puck sailed into the corner of the net for Steve's sixth point.

The Bobtails' fans roared, joining the thunder that rose from the boards against which Lines Two and Three were banging their sticks.

"Hey, man! Two hat tricks in one game! You're cooking!" sweaty-faced Eddie Traynor cried, smiling broadly as he skated up alongside of Steve.

Steve smiled back, his hazel eyes twinkling, his heart pounding under the blue shirt of his uniform. He wiped off the sweat that rolled down his own tired face and wished he didn't have to wear that hot helmet. But rules were rules.

"Just lucky," he said.

"Lucky, my eye," Eddie replied. "You're good, man."

"Thanks, Eddie," said Steve modestly.

Steve had learned to skate when he

4

was four years old. He had had a good teacher — his father. Edgar Crandall had played hockey in college and taught his young son to skate with hopes that someday he, too, would play college hockey.

But Steve's ability had turned out to be even better than Edgar Crandall had expected. "I think you would've turned out to be an excellent skater even if I hadn't taught you," he had told Steve one day. "Keep it up and someday you'll wind up as another Wayne Gretzky or Mike Bossy."

Steve knew of Gretzky and Bossy. They were two of the greatest hockey scorers ever. "That'll be the day, Dad," he said, grinning.

Steve had worked hard at being the best he could, hustling every minute, making every opportunity count, and — just as important — keeping himself in excellent physical condition by practicing constantly, eating well, and getting plenty of sleep. But the real key was his love of the game.

Line One of both teams played another minute, then relinquished the ice to the second lines. Steve, holding his helmet and stick, watched from behind the boards as both lines tried to score but didn't.

The Bobtails' Line Three did no better. They gave up one score fifty seconds before they got off the ice. Bobtails 6, Buckeyes 3.

Line One returned to the ice one last time. Feeling fresh and raring to go again, Steve, at center, gave the puck a hard poke as the referee dropped it at the blow of the whistle.

Jack Finlay, the Buckeyes' tall, bony center, struck the puck at the same time. Both hockey sticks clashed and clattered as they missed or connected with the puck. At last the disk shot across the Buckeyes' blue line where a Buckeye wingman hooked it with his stick

and sent it skittering toward a teammate at the other side of the rink. Rudy
Pollack, the Bobtails' defenseman, sped
after it and passed it to Jim Hogan, the
other Bobtails' defenseman.

But just then a husky Buckeye
crashed into him with a neat body check,
hooked his stick around the puck, and
carried it toward the Bobtails' goal.

He was fast and handled the puck
expertly. Steve, speeding across the blue
line after him, had a hunch that the
player intended to go for a score by himself.

Adding on an extra burst of speed,
Steve caught up to him just as the player
was about to take a hard swing at the
puck.

"Look out!" Steve yelled as he sped
past the player.

The Buckeye, his concentration dis-
rupted, paused for just an instant as he
glanced at Steve. Then he lashed out at
the puck. Too late. Steve grabbed it with
his stick as he flew by, skated in a half-

8

circle, then stickhandled the disk back up the ice. Two men raced after him. He passed to Eddie as a roar exploded from the Bobtails' fans, praising Steve for getting the puck back into Bobtails' possession.

Sweat beaded on Steve's lips and forehead. He took his time skating up the ice, remembering his father's wise advice to "reserve your energy at the right times." Yet, even when he was taking his time, he was almost as fast as some of the other players who were skating their fastest.

He took off with a burst of speed as left wingman Stu Pierce, receiving a pass from Eddie, bolted toward the net. Both of the Buckeyes' defensemen and their goalie put up a defensive wall against him.

"Stu!" Steve yelled as he skated up alongside of him.

Stu passed to him. Steve caught the puck, skated around the back of the net, and quickly passed it back to Stu. In a surprise move Stu stopped it with his stick, then flipped it toward the corner of the net, missing the goalie's right shoulder by inches.

Another score! This time Stu got the point and Steve the assist.

A call from Coach Larry Hall, standing behind the boards, was the signal for Line One to get off the ice and Line Two to replace them.

Four minutes later the game was over, with the Bobtails winning it 9 to 3.

Handshakes and shoulder pats greeted the Bobtails on their way to the locker room. After Steve showered and changed into his regular clothes he left the building, anxious to get home to fill his hunger-gnawing stomach. The late Saturday afternoon sun was slowly disappearing over the western horizon. The shadows were long, the November air crisp. The only signs of last week's snow were the white spots that clung to some roofs and corners the sun couldn't reach.

Steve, his blond hair still damp behind his neck, started to climb down the steps of Manley Rink when a boy about his age stepped up beside him. He was tall, well dressed, and wore leather gloves.

"Hi, Steve," he said, his brown eyes smiling. "I'm Mark Slate. You played a terrific game."

Steve frowned, bewildered. "Thanks," he said. Mark Slate? I don't know of any Mark Slate, he thought.

"I know you don't know me," Mark said, reading Steve's mind, "but I've watched you play in several games already, and . . . well . . . I feel almost as if I've known you for a long time."

"You've been watching *me* play? Why?" Steve looked again at the sharp clothes this Mark Slate wore, the expensive leather gloves. Something in the back of his mind began to creep into focus. He remembered now seeing Mark at some of the games, sitting in a seat on the top row, dressed very much as he was dressed now.

11

Mark's smile broadened. "For a good reason," he said. "And perfectly legitimate, believe me. Come on. I want to introduce you to a friend of mine, Kenneth Agard, Jr. He's over there, sitting in that car."

Steve looked at a shiny, black automobile parked at the curb, at the man sitting behind the wheel wearing a chauffeur's cap.

"You can't see Kenneth from here," said Mark. "He's sitting in the back seat."

He headed down the steps. Steve started to follow him, then paused. "I can't," he said.

Mark looked at him. "Why not? There's nothing to be afraid of. Kenneth is a good kid, and a genius when it comes to hockey. He just wants to talk —"

"I've got to get home," Steve cut in. "My parents are expecting me." He didn't want to say that they had warned him dozens of times not to trust strangers.

Mark must have heard that same warning dozens of times himself.

"Look, I know what you're thinking," Mark said. His voice was calm, friendly. "Don't trust strangers. Well, I don't blame you. But Kenneth Agard, Jr., is no stranger. He knows who you are, even though you don't know who he is. And he's as honest as the day is long. Take my word for it." He took Steve by the arm. "Come on. I guarantee you'll like him and what he has to tell you. I promise."

Steve studied Mark's face, saw the genuine look of friendliness in it, and felt as if he had known Mark a long time, too. Maybe I'm being too cautious, he thought. Mark seems like a real nice, trustworthy guy.

"Okay," Steve said. "I'll see your friend. But I can't stay long."

"Good," Mark said. "Come on."

Chapter 2

They got to the car, and Mark politely opened the rear door. "Kenneth, meet Steve Crandall," he said. "Steve, this is my friend, Kenneth Agard, Jr."

Steve barely heard him. He was looking at the shine on the limousine, at his reflection in it, then at the luxurious, bright-red interior. Boy, this Kenneth Agard guy must be *rich,* he thought.

His head was still swimming as he glanced at the boy in the back seat. Kenneth was dressed as neatly as Mark, but his smile, his well-groomed black

hair, and his brilliant brown eyes behind octagon-rimmed glasses, indicated to Steve that there was something special about him. Certainly nothing to distrust.

"Hi, Steve," Kenneth said, extending a hand. "I'm pleased to meet you. Come on, get in."

Steve remained standing, giving Kenneth a closer look. I can't believe it, he thought. He's not more than a year or so older than I am. Yet, he seems a lot older.

"Here, let me take your bag," said Mark.

Steve found himself handing the bag to Mark. Then he watched, wonderingly, as Mark carried it to the trunk of the car.

"Get in," Kenneth Agard, Jr., repeated. "We'll give you a lift home, and talk on the way. Okay?"

Steve put a foot inside the car. "Talk about what?"

"Hockey," Kenneth answered. "That's your favorite sport, isn't it?"

Steve was hardly aware that Kenneth was gently helping him into the car. He sat down beside Kenneth as he heard the trunk door slam shut. Then Mark came to the side of the car, closed the back seat door, and climbed in front with the driver. Instantly the car started up and eased away from the curb.

"I have an idea," Kenneth said. "We'll stop at a restaurant first. We'll eat, *then* we'll take you home. I'm sure you're hungry enough to eat a horse, right?" His eyes danced as he looked at Steve.

"No, I shouldn't," Steve said. "I have to get back home. My parents —"

"Don't worry about it," Kenneth broke in evenly. "Everything will be all right. Take my word for it. How does steak and onions sound to you?"

Steve shrugged. He hadn't had steak and onions in ages. "Good," he said. "But, really, I —"

17

Kenneth gave him a friendly pat. "Fine. The Tel-Man Restaurant, Mike," Kenneth said to the driver.

Steve's mouth was still open as he looked at Kenneth, then, as if in a daze, he gazed out the car window. This Agard guy certainly didn't let any grass grow under his feet, he thought. They drove outside of Water Falls and parked in front of the elegant Tel-Man Restaurant. Steve was familiar with it. He'd been there a few times with his parents, but *never* for steak.

They all got out of the car. Kenneth introduced the driver to Steve as simply "Mike, my chauffeur," then all four of them entered the restaurant. A waitress led them to a table, handed them each a menu, and said she'd be back in a minute.

"Order whatever you like," Kenneth said to Steve. "It's on me."

Steve stared at him. "I don't get it,"

he said, curious. "Why are you doing this?"

Kenneth smiled. "To get better acquainted. Why else?"

Why? thought Steve. Why should we get better acquainted?

The waitress returned. The boys and the chauffeur gave her their orders, then Kenneth talked about the Bobtails–Buckeyes hockey game. He was really impressed by Steve's performance, he said.

"You're even better than what the sports writers say about you," he said, his eyes flashing behind his glasses. "I'm more than an aficionado, Steve. My father was a college star, just like your father was. He taught me a lot about hockey, but mainly about the business end of it, which I'm mostly interested in."

Steve looked at him, feeling uncertain. Kenneth interested in the business end of hockey? Incredible. Wasn't that an adult's job? And then Steve remembered that Mark had said something about Kenneth being some kind of genius. Maybe it made sense. He wasn't sure.

Their dinners came. They ate, talking very little now. He seems to know a lot about me, Steve thought. And about my family.

When they finished, Kenneth paid the check with cash and left a sizable tip. "How do you feel now?" he asked Steve.

"Full," replied Steve. Is this it? he wondered. Did he take me to dinner just to tell me how impressed he was about my playing?

They left the restaurant and got back into the car. Steve couldn't remember ever having eaten so much steak and onions. He felt so full and contented he was sure he could fall asleep in five seconds if he closed his eyes.

It wasn't till a couple of minutes later

20

that he realized the car wasn't heading for Water Falls, but in the opposite direction. A cold chill rippled through him. What was Kenneth up to? He had promised to give me a lift home, Steve thought, glancing aside at the boy genius sitting next to him.

"Where are we going now?" he wanted to know. All at once he was nervous, frightened. Kenneth hadn't said that they'd be going anywhere else.

"We're going to the airport, Steve," said Kenneth, as calmly as if he were talking about the weather. "And then flying to Indiana. Now, just take it easy. There's nothing to worry about, I promise you. If it'll make you feel any better, your parents know about this and are totally agreeable to your coming with me."

Steve stared at him. Kenneth seemed so *decent,* Steve thought, but was that decency just make-believe? How could he know?

"Why can't I see them first?" he asked, the chill gripping his spine getting even colder.

"Because we don't have time," Kenneth said. He took a letter out of his pocket and handed it to Steve. "Here, read it," he said. "It's from your father to me."

Steve took the letter, unfolded it, and saw that it had been typed. It could've been written by anybody, he thought. But the signature below it was definitely his father's.

Dear Mr. Agard, Jr., (he read)

> *Thanks for your very kind words about our son Steve. We feel that he has potential as a future hockey star, too, and my wife and I are in complete agreement in permitting him to go with you to Indiana for further development. Providing a private school for his education solves that problem, indeed. However, although we have signed the agreement, whether or not he goes is his decision.*

Your pay offer is generous, and we will see to it that it goes into a special trust fund for Steve, providing he accepts your offer, of course.

Best wishes,
Edgar Crandall

Steve stared at Kenneth. Letter or not, something seemed fishy about this whole thing, he thought. That signature *looked* like his father's, but it could have been forged. Another thing: why hadn't his parents said anything to him about this? They must have known before today's game about the deal Kenneth Agard, Jr., had planned for him.

"No! I won't go with you!" he shouted, shaking the letter at Kenneth. "How do I know you're not kidnappers? What're you going to do? Send a ransom note — "

"No, no, no," Kenneth said, grabbing the letter away from Steve. "You're letting your imagination run away with

23

you. Just a minute. Let me show you something."

While Kenneth reached into the briefcase beside him, Mark Slate said, "Steve, I told you not to worry. Please trust us. We're not kidnapping you, or anything crazy like that. Kenneth has just recognized a potential hockey star in you and wants to do all he can in developing it, that's all."

"Sure," said Steve. "If I believe that, I'd believe anything."

"Then *believe*," Kenneth Agard, Jr., said, as he handed Steve a book he'd taken from his briefcase. It was a scrapbook, filled with articles about Steve's team — more than he knew ever existed — and photographs of Steve taking swiping shots at a puck, each one different, showing his aggressiveness, ability, and love for the game.

Steve looked at them, stunned. "Who took these pictures?" he asked.

"I did," Mark said, and grinned. "Now do you believe?"

"I — I'm not sure," Steve said.

He handed the scrapbook back to Kenneth, leaned back, and gazed out of the window. Those articles and pictures of him were genuine, all right. Strong evidence that Kenneth Agard, Jr., was sincere in his appreciation of Steve's hockey playing ability. But did that mean he could take Steve away like this? Take him to Indiana?

They finally arrived at the airport. It was so small it boasted only two runways. Mike, the chauffeur, entered the small terminal building and emerged a few minutes later with a piece of paper he put into his jacket pocket. Then all four of them walked to a sleek, white, twin-engined jet airplane parked alongside two smaller airplanes and got in.

Mike sat at the controls, Mark beside him. Steve and Kenneth sat behind them. They fastened their seatbelts and Mike started up the engines. After a few sputtering coughs the engines began to run smoothly. The plane taxied down the runway and in a minute it was airborne.

"Where exactly are we going to in Indiana?" Steve asked, glancing at Kenneth.

"The name of the town makes no difference. The place does," Kenneth answered. "It's the biggest, most beautiful ice rink you'll ever see."

Chapter 3

Less than an hour later Steve felt a slight bump and the *zip-zip* sound of the tires as the plane landed on a private airport in country surroundings. He was still baffled by what was happening to him, as if this were all a dream. A bad nightmare. Maybe he'd wake up and find that it *was* a dream. But he knew better. It was real. It was all too real.

Mike taxied the plane into a hangar that housed a smaller plane, and everyone got out and into a car that was parked outside. Mike started it, and drove across the runway to a macadam road, speeding ahead with headlights piercing the fast falling darkness.

In less than five minutes they slowed down, drove into a long, tree-flanked private driveway, and parked in front of a white, colonial mansion. Steve saw that only the right side of the building had its lights turned on.

"That's the side occupied by the Chariots, our hockey team," Kenneth explained. "They sleep, eat, play games, and watch television there. When they're not playing hockey, that is," he added, grinning.

As Mike drove off with the car, Kenneth, Mark, and Steve walked up to the large front door. Kenneth rapped the brass knocker against the panel and a moment later the door was opened by a tall, middle-aged man whose head was as bald and shiny as a peeled egg.

"Master Kenneth!" he greeted jovially. "We've been expecting you! Hello, Mark."

"Hello, Andrew," Kenneth and Mark both said. "This is our new member, Steve Crandall," Kenneth went on. "Are his quarters all set up, Andrew?"

"Oh, you bet, sir," replied Andrew, smiling. Steve stared at him, then at "Master Kenneth." My quarters all set up? I can't believe this! Steve thought. Kenneth had reneged on his word from the very beginning! He had said he wouldn't take me with him unless I agreed to go. Well, I *haven't* agreed!

Steve's heart pounded as he saw Andrew extending a hand out to him. "Glad to meet you, Steve," Andrew was saying. "I'm sure you'll enjoy it very much here. Come in, come in. Here, let me take your bag."

"It's just my hockey uniform and skates," Steve explained, automatically handing it to him.

Andrew's gray eyes danced. "I know. It usually is, my boy."

Kenneth chuckled. "Andrew's quite an amusing fellow," he said. "You'll find that he's a lot of fun around here."

I wonder, Steve thought, feeling his skin prickle. He followed Andrew up a spiral staircase and through a door that opened into a large room equipped with several cots. Five, Steve counted, as he thought: cots? I've never slept on a cot in my life! Next to each cot was a chair, a desk, and a desk lamp. Pictures, which covered the peach-painted walls, ranged from astronauts on the moon to hockey players on ice.

"Your cot is number five, Steve," said Andrew, placing the bag on it. "I'll leave you in Mark's custody now. He'll tell you what to do. Good night."

"Good night," Steve heard himself say. He watched Andrew leave and saw Mark standing at the side of the doorway. "What is this, Mark?" he asked.

30

"Everybody seems to think I'm really going to stay here."

"Well, no one is sure of that yet, of course," Mark replied, coming closer. "But we're going to try our best. You're a fine hockey player, Steve, and you might as well face it. Kenneth is going to do everything he can to make you *want* to stay here and play with the Chariots. Well, almost everything," he added, smiling. "A private room, for example. Nobody has one here, except Kenneth. Anyway, he just started the team this year and has already made it the best professional kid's hockey team in the country."

Steve frowned. "Professional?"

"That's right. Professional. We schedule games with the best teams and demand a certain fee. Sometimes we get it, sometimes we don't. But it's always substantial, enough for Kenneth to keep putting money into each of our trust funds as he promised."

31

"Is he really the head of the Chariots, or is he working for someone else? His father, say."

"Well, he's co-owner with his father," said Mark. "But he runs the Chariots. He's the brains. And he's got them, believe me. Would you believe he's already graduated from college?"

Steve's eyebrows arched. "But he can't be more than thirteen!" he said, incredulous.

"He isn't. But he's brilliant. What's more, he knows as much about hockey as he does math, which he majored in. I'm telling you, Steve, every guy here is really honored by having been picked to play for the Chariots. Not one of them has ever been sorry. I'll warn you: he'll work you hard. You're going to have to practice your tail off, but it'll pay off, because you'll find that you're playing on the best kid's hockey team in the country with good possibilities of joining a professional hockey team in three or four years. Can you think of anything that is more promising than that for kids our age? I'm telling you, I can't."

"I still don't like this," Steve insisted, dropping hard on one of the cots, clamping his hands into fists. "I still feel like I've been kidnapped."

"Steve." Mark came toward him, put a hand on Steve's shoulder. "You're wrong. Believe me. You weren't kidnapped. You were just brought here for the chance of a lifetime to show your ability. You don't think Kenneth's father would let Kenneth get away with a dangerous thing like kidnapping, do you?"

I don't know, Steve wanted to say. I don't know Kenneth's father.

"What does his father do?" Steve asked.

"Mr. Agard is president of the Blue Gills hockey team. It's Kenneth's hope that some of us will become good enough to play on it when we're too old to play with the Chariots."

"When is 'too old?' "

"When we turn sixteen," Mark answered.

"How old are you, Mark?"

"Fourteen."

"Where are you from?"

"California?"

"California?" Steve frowned. "How long have you been here?"

"Almost a year. I'm a charter member." Mark rubbed his palms together and smiled. "Well, we've shot the breeze long enough. Come on downstairs and I'll introduce you to the guys."

Steve met them all, including the two players with whom, Mark told him, he was going to be teamed up on Line One: Hal Spoon and Nick Troy. Providing he decided to stay, Mark added as an afterthought.

Steve noticed a large desk to the right of the door as one entered the room, and the big broad-shouldered man who sat behind it. Another man was sitting on a settee, reading a newspaper. Both men seemed preoccupied, yet Steve had a feeling that neither one of them was missing a thing that went on in the room.

Curfew was at ten o'clock, when the lights dimmed, some of them turning off completely.

Back in the room upstairs Steve saw that both Hal Spoon and Nick Troy were his roommates. The other two were Mark Slate and Ray Hutchings. Steve was glad that Mark was a roommate, too, mainly because Mark was the only one among the guys Steve knew. Maybe after he got acquainted with some of the other guys he could gain the confidence of at least one of them and find out the *real* story behind all this. Had all these guys been duped to come here as he had been? he wondered. Could be. Not one of them looked happy. Everyone he'd seen so far looked as if he were in a world of his own. What kind of hold had Kenneth Agard, Jr., on them, anyway?

"Your locker's number five, Steve," Mark said as he sat down and started to remove his shoes. "You'll find your 'jamas in there, plus a new outfit of clothes."

Steve looked at him, surprised. "New outfit of clothes?" he echoed. "Suppose they don't fit?"

"If they don't, we'll get you ones that will." Mark smiled. "Sleep tight, Steve. Classes are from nine to twelve, then we'll have a hockey scrimmage in the afternoon. So you'll want a good rest. Good night."

"Good night," Steve replied, staring at Mark as if he were already dreaming as he crawled into bed.

36

Chapter 4

Steve and his roommates were awak-
ened at seven o'clock by a soft tapping
on the door. He showered, then dressed
in his new clothes, finding them to fit
him almost perfectly. How did Kenneth
Agard, Jr., do it? he wondered. Did he
get my measurements from Mom and
Dad?

Breakfast was at seven-thirty in the
cafeteria next to the recreation room,
but Steve didn't feel hungry. He missed
home. He missed his mother and father.

He finally forced down a biscuit and half a glass of milk.

Steve noticed again the two men he had seen last night. They were standing near the door, talking to each other, apparently oblivious of the twenty-five boys sitting at the three long tables. Yet Steve suspected that there wasn't a thing going on in the room that escaped their attention.

They are probably here to maintain order, he thought. Why else would they be here?

The boys had a break between eight and nine o'clock. At ten minutes of nine a buzzer sounded and the boys got up and started to leave. Steve stared curiously after them until Mark, who had been sitting with him, Hal, and Nick, said, "Stay here, Steve. We're going after our workbooks. I'll get yours."

"Okay."

In a few minutes the boys returned, each carrying a workbook and pencil.

38

Mark handed Steve his. "Here you are," he said. "This is all we get, so just listen carefully to your instructor and do as he says. We're put in classes according to our ages. You're thirteen, so you're in Group A. See you at noon."

Steve nodded, feeling slightly numb from the quick pace of things.

"Come on, Steve," said Hal. "I'm in Group A, too."

Steve followed him across the room and sat at the table in front of which a sign on the wall read: GROUP A. Altogether six boys made up the group, indicating that there were more fourteen- and fifteen-year-old kids than thirteen-year-olds.

Group A's instructor was Roger Harlan, one of the men Steve had seen in the building. Mr. Harlan, six foot four, dark-haired, built like a football tackle, exchanged introductions with Steve, then took a minute to explain about the subjects.

"We have three one-hour classes each day," he said. "English, math, and social sciences are taught on Mondays, Wednesdays, and Fridays; earth sciences, lab, and Spanish on Tuesdays and Thursdays."

"I don't care about that," Steve said, looking directly into Mr. Harlan's dark brown eyes. "I'm only here for the day."

Harlan smiled. Steve cringed. The smile reminded him of a cobra he had seen once at a zoo. Mr. Harlan went on as if he hadn't heard a word Steve said. "We don't use books, only those workbooks in which you take notes. I suggest you keep your eyes and ears open and write only those parts of my lectures which you think are important."

Steve glanced behind him, wondering if Kenneth might have come into the room. *If he thinks he's going to keep me here longer than one day, he's crazy,* Steve thought. But Kenneth wasn't anywhere to be seen. Finally Mr. Harlan's droning ended. Steve picked up his books and followed Mark and the other boys to the classrooms.

After classes were over, Hal asked him, "Well? How do you like our school?"

"I don't," Steve answered. "I want out . . . *now*."

"Why don't you wait till you skate on our rink and get a feel of our kind of hockey?" a voice cut in at his elbow. "You might change your mind."

Steve looked around at Mark. "I doubt it," he said. But the thought of getting into a hockey uniform and onto the rink intrigued him. What do the Chariots have that I haven't seen before? he wondered. Maybe he could wait at least long enough to find out, he thought, *then* see Kenneth and lay it on the line that he definitely wanted out. And make his decision stick.

The boys rested for an hour after dinner, then got into their hockey uniforms and rode a bus five miles to the coliseum

41

in the city where, Mark explained, the Blue Gills played their local hockey games. Here, also, the Chariots practiced and played their games.

Steve couldn't help but be impressed by the oval building and the banners that hung from the ceiling, each with the name of a professional hockey team printed on it. The rink was milk-white, the blue and red lines on the ice were like brand-new, bright ribbons.

The players removed the protective rubber from their skates and got on the ice, each one with a hockey stick. Kenneth Agard, Jr., sat in the area reserved for the scorekeeper and reporters, and watched the players skate around the rink for about five minutes before barking his first order.

"All right. We're going to begin scrimmage. Here are the players for Line One defending the goal to my right. Put on white jerseys as I call your names. Goalie, Jason Moore; right defense, Ray

Hutchings; left defense, Mark Slate; center, Steve Crandall; right wingman, Hal Spoon; left wingman, Nick Troy. Line Two — no uniform change for you guys. Goalie, Chick Culligan; right defense, Andy Messenger; left defense, Tony Morris; center, Jack Potter; right wingman, Mel Hale; left wingman, Harvey Malone. All other players please leave the ice."

Steve, his heart pounding after he got his jersey from the pile on the bench, skated to the face-off circle and waited for his opponent, Jack Potter, to get in position in front of him. Jack was a couple of inches taller than he, and a few pounds heavier, but Steve dismissed the difference in their sizes. He was in his element now. This was hockey, and an opponent's size didn't matter. He could be a giant as far as Steve was concerned. *This is my game and I'm going to play it to the hilt*, Steve thought.

The referee — a tall, bald-headed man

Steve had seen in the recreation hall —
blew his whistle, then dropped the puck.
Steve and Jack struck at it simultaneously, moving the disk in short,
snappy jerks every which way until a
hard thrust by Steve sent it scurrying
across the ice. Hal got it, stickhandled
it toward the goal, then passed it to Nick.
Instantly both of Line Two's defensemen charged at Nick. One of them
bodychecked him hard just as he passed
the puck toward Steve.

Jack sped past Steve, his stick held
out in front of him. Quickly Steve dug
his skates into the ice and swung in
front of Jack, his stick hitting Jack's
away then grabbing the puck. He hooked
it smoothly, stealing it completely from
his opponent, and drawing a surprised
and angry look from him.

As Steve stickhandled the puck he
looked for an opening behind the
crouching goalie, saw one, and shot.
Slap! The goalie jerked up his right arm

in an effort to stop the puck, but missed it by a mile. Goal!

"Nice shooting, Steve!" Kenneth yelled.

Mark skated up beside him. "Beautiful flip-shot, Steve," he said, smiling.

"Thanks," said Steve, smiling back. *This is even easier than I thought, Mark, ol' buddy,* he wanted to say.

As Steve returned to the face-off circle he saw that Jack Potter wasn't as appreciative. Jack's eyes were cold, his jaw set.

The whistle shrilled; the puck dropped. Both centers' sticks cracked like whips as the boys fought for control of the puck. Suddenly Jack spun on both skates, knocking Steve aside, and took possession. Steve stared, surprised, as Jack took off down the ice with the puck, then passed it to a teammate.

Not wasting another second, Steve, anger flushing his cheeks, bolted down the ice. Quickly he saw a play in the making: Mel Hale, Line Two's right wingman, was wide open near the side of the rink and Jack was skating down center ice. Mel seemed to be the logical player to pass to.

Steve headed for him. A second later Jack passed the puck to Mel. Steve, skating with all the speed he could muster, reached out his stick, grabbed the puck, stopped, then shot it across the ice to Roy. The defenseman caught it, controlled it until his teammates had crossed the blue line, then fired it to Nick. In a wild scramble Nick lost it to Jack who again raced with it to the side of the rink, then down along the boards toward his goal.

Steve, hot on his heels, got near enough to Jack to reach for the puck. This time Jack shot it toward the goal, swinging the stick hard and carelessly. Steve winced as it struck him on the side. He was sure that Jack had done it on purpose, but he controlled his temper.

He started to sprint down the ice but had hardly taken two steps when Jack, glancing over his shoulder, bolted in front of him. Their skates collided. Steve, unable to hold his balance, fell.

A corner of Jack's mouth curved into a grin as he yanked his skate free from Steve's and bolted away. Steve scrambled to his feet, anger boiling inside of him. He'd be darned if he'd let Jack get away with that!

He sprinted across the ice where Harvey, Roy, and Jack were fighting for control of the puck. Suddenly Jack yanked it free and started to stickhandle it down the ice toward his goal. He didn't see Steve coming after him until the very last instant when he suddenly swerved, carrying the puck with him. Steve, seeing an opportunity for a good bodycheck, charged into the tall center.

Steve felt the impact of his body striking Jack's. Then both of them slid across the ice, Jack swinging his stick around as an angry snarl tore from him. Not sure whether the center intended to strike him with it or not, Steve didn't take any chances. He grabbed Jack's arm and held it for a moment before he let it go, quite certain by then that Jack wouldn't use it against him.

Jack didn't. But the grim look on his face was unmistakable.

"Okay!" Kenneth yelled. "Line One, off the ice! Give Line Three your jerseys!"

As Steve pulled off his jersey and skated off the ice, he glanced at Kenneth Agard, Jr., and saw a whimsical smile come over the young coach's face.

"Well, how does it feel?" Kenneth said. "Great, right?"

"I guess." Steve took a deep breath, and exhaled it. "Can I see you a minute? It's . . . it's important."

48

"Not now, Steve. I'm busy now — you can see that." Kenneth turned his attention back to the practice game and immediately started to yell to Line Three, "Get moving, you guys! Get moving!"

He's brushing me off, Steve thought. But I'm going to tell him what's on my mind. He's not going to brush me off for long.

Chapter 5

The team scrimmaged for an hour, then showered and rode back to their quarters, tired and hungry.

Mark, sitting with Steve in the bus as it breezed along smoothly on the winding country road, broke the awkward silence between them. "You really looked good, Steve," he said. "Kenneth was quite impressed."

"I saw that he was," said Steve, remembering his smile.

Hal Spoon looked back at them from the seat ahead and grinned, the first time that Steve remembered seeing

50

anything else on Hal's long, slender face besides a sad, somber look. "I think that you showed Jack up, too," he said. "You looked great."

"Thanks, Hal," replied Steve. "But I just didn't want to let him get away with what he was doing, that's all."

Hal's grin broadened. "I figured that," he said, and turned back around.

Steve rested his head back against the seat and closed his eyes. Almost instantly his mother and father came into his thoughts, and a loneliness hit him. He had never been away from them for more than a couple of days. Nor had there ever been more than twenty miles separating them. Now he was in another state and there were over five or six hundred miles between them.

He opened his eyes. "Mark."

"Yeah?"

"I haven't had a chance to tell Kenneth that I don't want to stay. Would you try to see him for me?"

Mark looked at him. "You've been

51

with us just a little while, Steve," he said. "Give yourself more time to think about it."

"I don't need more time," Steve answered. "I want to go home, Mark."

Mark rested his head back, said nothing.

"You heard me, didn't you, Mark?" said Steve. "I said I want to go home."

"Yes, I heard you," Mark said.

"Well?"

"You can't go back, Steve. Not right away."

Steve sat up. "Who's going to stop me? If I want to go back I'll *go* back. Neither you, Kenneth, nor anyone else is going to stop me."

"Sorry, Steve," said Mark calmly. "But you are *not* going back. You might as well face up to that fact now."

Steve's face paled. "You mean that I — I'm like a prisoner?"

Mark shook his head. "It's not like that at all, Steve. It's just that once

Kenneth gets a kid he thinks is really a top-notch hockey player, he's going to keep him. And he thinks you're top-notch, Steve. I know he won't want to let you go."

"That's crazy!" Steve cried. "Who does he think he is, anyway?"

"Calm down, Steve. Everyone's staring."

"Let them stare. Just because they're all dumb enough to stay here . . ."

"Sssh!" said Hal, turning to look back at Steve. "The driver's got his eyes on you."

Steve glanced at the rearview mirror and saw the hard, staring eyes of the driver fixed on him. His heart pounded as he fell back against the seat and stared at the ceiling of the bus.

I must be having a nightmare, he thought. This can't really be happening.

Steve looked for Kenneth during dinnertime, but the young team co-owner and coach was nowhere around. He didn't sit down to eat with the team, anyway, Steve learned. He sat in another part of the house with his parents.

What kind of parents does he have to let him practically have the run of the place? Steve wondered. And what kind of kid was Kenneth, really? Brilliant, yes. And an expert in hockey. But he was more than that. He was a *monster*.

"I'd like to write a letter to my parents," Steve said to Mark after dinner. "Can I have some stationery?"

Mark shook his head. "Sorry, Steve. Nobody writes any letters here."

Steve couldn't believe it. "Why not? Don't you think that our parents want to know what we're doing?"

"Kenneth keeps them in touch," he said. "Don't worry. If anything happens back home, you'll know about it right away. And if anything happens to you, your parents will be notified."

"Why can't *we* write to our parents?" Steve insisted.

"Kenneth believes that by not writing letters the guys won't get homesick," Mark answered. "And it's proven true. I've been here almost a year now and I haven't been homesick at all. You'll get used to it after a while. All the guys feel the same way."

"Well, I don't," said Steve harshly. "I love my parents, and I think they'd want to hear from me."

"They don't expect to," said Mark. "Kenneth explained it to them, and they were agreeable. Honestly, Steve," Mark added, smiling that warm, genial smile of his, "what practical purpose would there be by writing letters to your parents? You'd just think about them more, and get homesick. Your playing might suffer, too. Think about it, Steve. There is no organization for young hockey players in the country that is run so expertly and successfully as this one.

55

It's a professional farm team. The big leagues have them, but their players are older than we are, and are in leagues. We aren't. Our games are exhibitions, and we fly all over the country to play the best teams that could be put up against us." His eyes danced. "Know what? Kenneth is considering scheduling games with some of the European countries."

"I can't believe it," said Steve.

"Well, believe it," Mark said, his eyes sparkling. "I tell you, that kid's a genius."

"He's a monster," Steve said softly.

Mark chuckled. "That's what I thought, too, when he brought me here," he said. "But I've changed my tune. You might as well change yours, too, Steve. It won't do you any good to fight Kenneth."

"I can try running away."

Mark looked at him. "Steve, what do your parents do?"

"My father — he's a technician in a hospital."

"How much does he earn?"

"I don't know." Steve looked hard at Mark. "Never mind. I know what you're trying to say. We can use the extra money."

Mark smiled. "Right. Come on. Let's take in tonight's video. It's an oldie. A cowboy picture."

Reluctantly, Steve followed Mark upstairs into a room where the videos were shown. Several boys were already there, waiting for the movie to start. Others kept dribbling in until, promptly at seven-thirty, the movie started.

It turned out to be one that Steve had not seen before. But throughout the picture his mind reverted to his mother and father. It just didn't seem possible, he thought, that they would agree with Kenneth Agard, Jr., about not writing to, or receiving letters from, their son.

57

Chapter 6

Early on Wednesday morning the team
rode by bus to the airport and jet-lined
to Philadelphia. They were accompanied by their young coach, Kenneth
Agard, Jr., and two chaperones, Mr.
Healy and Mr. Karpis, who were grim-
faced, hard-looking men. Steve wanted
desperately to talk to Kenneth, but he
didn't dare. Not with Mr. Healy and Mr.
Karpis around.

They played that evening in the same
rink where the Flyers played. Steve,
skating around it during the pre-game

warm up, looked with nervousness and surprise at the fans streaming in through the entranceways. Never before had he played in front of a crowd as large as this one was going to be.

The Angels' white satin uniforms, trimmed in light blue, were a sharp contrast to the Chariots' red ones. Steve didn't know much about the Angels except that they were good. Kenneth would not have scheduled a game with them if they weren't, that's for sure.

At seven-twenty the whistle blew, signaling the players to get off the ice. At seven-twenty-five it blew again, signaling the first lines of both teams to get back on it. The crowd cheered. An announcer named all positions and more cheers went up.

"The game will be divided into three periods of eighteen minutes each," the announcer explained. "Each line will play two minutes three times a period.

There will be a ten-minute break in between periods."

In the center face-off circle Steve found himself facing a fair-skinned, brown-eyed boy about his height and slightly thinner. The boy's name was Dick Wirtz. Steve thought: *This is going to be like taking candy from a kid.*

The puck dropped. The whistle shrilled. Sticks clashed as both centers tried to get control of the puck. Suddenly both sticks hooked together and Steve discovered the powerful strength of his opponent's hands. For one fraction of a second he glanced up, met Dick's eyes squarely, and saw in them the defiance and aggressiveness of a fearless hockey player. Steve's first impression of Dick Wirtz changed. He had a feeling that if Dick was like this, so were most of the other Angels.

Their sticks broke loose and Dick whacked the puck, driving it toward center ice. An Angels' wingman caught the pass and carried it across the Chariots' blue line, his skates biting into the ice as he raced across it. Steve sprinted after him, heading directly toward the Chariots' goal where Jason Moore crouched in the crease, his eyes like black holes in his white mask.

The Angels' wingman tried a slap shot as he sped toward the net. The puck headed for the corner next to Jason's left foot, but the goalie stopped it with his stick and shoved it to Mark Slate as the defenseman skated up beside him.

"Nice save, Jason," said Mark who, Steve had noticed, always had a good word for every guy on the team. He was a regular one-man cheerleading squad.

Mark stickhandled the disk around the back of the net, then passed it to Steve who carried it up along the boards. An Angels' defenseman came pell-mell after him, fierce determination shining in his eyes. Just as Steve shot a pass across the ice toward Nick, the defenseman struck the Chariots' center, checking him into the boards.

Shreeeek!

"Boarding!" called the referee, and the game was stopped as the penalized Angel skated off the ice.

During the minute that the Angel sat in the penalty box the Chariots played their hearts out to score. Twice Steve took shots at the Angels' net, only to have the Angels' goalie catch the puck in his gloved hands both times.

It was after the penalized player returned to the ice that a scoring play seemed to be in the making for the Angels. Dick Wirtz had the puck in his possession, stickhandling it down the middle of the ice with his wingmen on either side of him. Roy and Mark stopped in front of their net, helping Jason defend it. From the wings came Hal and Nick, and coming up behind Dick was Steve.

"Take the wingmen!" Steve shouted.

Both Hal and Nick glanced at him with puzzled looks on their faces.

"Take them!" Steve shouted again.

As he yelled he saw the wingmen look over their shoulders. At the same time he dug his skates into the ice, sprinting around the right wingman in a move so swift that it confused the Angel. As the wingman turned to follow him, Nick checked him, throwing him off-balance and giving Steve the opportunity to go after the puck carrier.

Dick was within eight feet of the goal when he reared his stick back and started to bring it down in a hard slap-shot swing. Skating with all the power he could muster, Steve came abreast of the Angels' center's side and reached out his stick. Just as Dick's stick came down in a sweeping arc, Steve grabbed the puck, swept around in an ice-flying circle, and headed back in the opposite direction. A roar burst from the fans as he stickhandled the puck down the ice, not an Angel in front of him except the goaltender.

Skating across center ice and then over the blue line into Angels' territory, he looked at the net for a target. The goalie was crouched in front of it, covering the middle, gloved hand and stick ready.

Steve headed for him, the sound of fast-approaching, singing blades behind him. When he was almost four feet from the crease, Steve changed the position of his hands on the stick, swung to the left, and shot. Whack! The puck skittered through the hole between the goalie's out-swinging stick and the edge of the net.

Goal! Thunder boomed from the fans. Sticks clattered against the boards as the Chariots expressed their approval.

"Nice shot, Steve!" Mark said as he and the other members of the Chariots' line swarmed around him.

Steve skated slowly toward the neutral zone, breathing tiredly. As he wiped at the sweat that drizzled down his face someone brushed hard against his elbow. He looked at the player. It was Dick Wirtz.

Steve ignored him.

Face-off. The puck dropped, the whistle blew, and Dick's stick was a fraction of a second ahead of Steve's at the puck. The disk shot across the ice to an Angels' wingman who carried it toward center ice. Steve, swinging around to go after the puck, felt his skate being hooked by the blade of another skate. As if someone had yanked his leg from under him, he fell. A chuckle rippled from the offender, Dick Wirtz, and Steve saw the center skate past him.

But no whistle blew. The ref hadn't seen Dick pull the violation.

Steve scrambled to his feet and took off down the middle of the ice, anger rising in him. He wasn't looking for revenge, though. He was looking for the puck.

Suddenly a horn buzzed. The first two minutes were up. The lines of both teams skated off the ice. Their second lines skated on.

Steve was bushed as he sat down. He took the towel handed to him by one of the guys, wiped his face with it, then passed it to the next player.

In a little while he felt better. His heart stopped pounding. The cool air of the huge room freshened his face.

He looked at the crowd. The place was jam-packed.

Chick Culligan, the Chariots' Line Two goalie, had three saves within the first minute, then missed a high-flying shot for the Angels' first score. Chariots 1, Angels 1.

The Angels' Line Three garnered another score to go into the lead, 2 to 1.

"Let's get 'em," said Mark as the buzzer sounded and Line One scrambled back on the ice.

Refreshed from the rest, Steve felt more comfortable and less nervous now

67

than the first time he was on the ice. Within seconds he stole the puck from an Angels' wingman and was moving it down toward center ice. As he crossed the red line he saw a blue-uniformed player creeping up on him at his left side. Steve knew that a bodycheck was ready to come. But he wasn't about to accept it.

Stopping almost on the spot and hooking the blade of his stick around the puck, he saw the player whisk by him. It was Dick Wirtz. Dick reached his stick out to grab the puck, but caught Steve's stick instead. A quick, sudden yank, catching Steve by surprise, pulled the stick out of Steve's hand and flung it across the ice.

Mouth opened as he stared at Dick, Steve felt a moment of intense embarrassment. Never had anyone ever yanked a hockey stick out of his hand before.

Chapter 7

His face red, Steve bolted after the stick and scooped it off the ice. He glanced around and saw that Dick still had control of the puck and was carrying it up the ice toward the Chariots' goal.

"That-a-way, kid! Don't let him get away with it!" a fan shouted, then laughed hilariously.

Very funny, thought Steve as he shot across the red line into Chariots' territory.

Dick crossed the blue line and shot a pass to a wingman as Mark sped up to him and checked him hard with his hip.

Dick swung his stick around as he spun to keep his balance, and almost hit Steve. The loose puck skidded toward the boards, and Steve skated after it. He, Mark, and an Angels' defenseman reached it at the same time.

Mark jammed the man against the boards, holding him there until Steve got the puck. As Steve turned he saw Dick bolting toward him, eyes flashing anger.

With a snap of his stick Steve passed the puck to Hal, and Hal stickhandled it across center ice with no one near him. Steve crouched and dug his skates hard in swift pursuit, then crashed to the ice as Dick's skate rammed into one of his. Stunned, Steve slid across the ice, colliding into Roy and knocking him off balance.

Hal got within four feet of the net and shot. The puck never got past the crease as the Angels' goaltender stopped it with his glove.

Neither line scored. And, after each line completed its third session on the ice, Steve was glad that break-time had come. The score was still 2 to 1 in the Angels' favor.

As both teams headed to their respective locker rooms, someone touched Steve's arm. Steve glanced around. It was Hal.

"I'd like to talk to you, Steve," Hal said in a low voice.

Steve frowned. "About what?"

"About —" Hal's eyes suddenly focused on someone beyond Steve, and he hesitated. "Later," he said.

Steve looked over his left shoulder and saw Mark behind him. What was Hal going to say, he thought, that he didn't want Mark to hear?

They sat on benches in the locker room, their helmets on the floor between their feet. Steve looked across the room at Hal, but the wingman was resting back against a locker, his eyes closed.

Standing near the door were the two men who had accompanied the team, Mr. Healy and Mr. Karpis. They weren't just chaperones, Steve thought. They were *guards*. He and the rest of the team were their prisoners.

Kenneth Agard, Jr., entered the room with a smile and a basketful of oranges.

"Good game so far, men," he said, his eyes partially hidden behind his octagon-rimmed glasses. His smile faded slightly. "But you've got to do better. Only one goal in the first period is ridiculous."

He gave them each an orange, which they peeled and ate. When Steve glanced again at Hal he met Hal's eyes. He was sure they were trying to tell him something.

A few minutes later, when the teams were back on the ice for a brief warm up before the second period, Steve glided up beside Hal.

"What did you want to say to me, Hal?" he asked softly.

"Never mind," said Hal. His eyes darted nervously around the rink.

"But you said you wanted to talk to me."

Hal's face darkened. "I changed my mind," he said stiffly. "Quit bugging me, okay?"

Steve looked at him, puzzled, then skated away. A couple of minutes later the buzzer sounded. The second period was ready to begin.

Hal's got something on his mind, Steve thought. I wish he'd tell me what it is.

Face-off. This time Steve grabbed the puck, then almost tripped over Dick's right skate. He caught his balance and saw Hal grab the puck and pass it to Nick. Nick raced with it across the blue line into the neutral zone, then passed it to Mark. A whistle shrilled, and Steve saw that Mark had had his left foot behind the Chariots' blue line when Hal had passed the puck to him, an off-side violation.

Face-off between Nick and an An-

73

gels' forward. The forward grabbed the puck and passed it to Dick, who headed down the middle of the ice. In a second Steve was hot on his tail. Oblivious of the fast approaching center, Dick seemed to be ignoring his wingman as he raced toward the goal.

Steve put on an extra burst of speed, caught up to Dick, and checked him with his hip. The blow knocked Dick off balance; made him lose control of the puck. Grabbing the disk with the blade of his stick, Steve turned and headed back up the ice. As both of the Angels' wingmen tore after him, he passed the puck to Mark. Mark stickhandled it toward the neutral zone and across the blue line. Blocked by a defenseman, Mark brought himself up short, ice spraying from his skates. For an instant he stood there, his stick guarding the puck as he looked around quickly for someone to pass to. Sweat shone on his face.

Dick came up unexpectedly behind him, checked the Chariots' defenseman on the left hip, and knocked him to the ice. Then Dick grabbed the puck, but Steve, bolting by him, hit his stick, stole the puck, and in the same swift motion shot it toward the net. The surprised goalie, caught off-guard, saw the puck flying across the ice toward him too late to be able to stop it.

Goal! Chariots 2, Angels 2.

Steve, skating slowly back toward the center circle as the Chariots' bench thundered their approval of his shot and of the score, cut toward Hal and said, "Hal! Are you going to tell me what you wanted to see me about?"

"No!" Hal answered. "Forget it, will you?"

Steve frowned, then skated to the face-off circle. I wonder what he wanted to tell me, Steve thought, and why he's changed his mind. Is he afraid somebody else might know what he wanted to say? But who? Mark? Was Hal afraid that Mark might then tell Kenneth whatever it was he wanted to say?

75

Again Steve grabbed the face-off. Seconds later he saw Hal carrying the puck down center ice, no one near him except an Angels' defenseman. Hal evaded him easily, bolted straight for the net, then cut sharply to the right. Steve watched expectantly.

"Shoot, Hal! Shoot!" he cried.

Steve had barely gotten the words out of his mouth when Hal shot. The puck streaked past the Angels' goalie's right foot into the net. It was 3 to 2, the Chariots' favor.

"Good shot, Hal!" Steve shouted. Well, whatever was on Hal's mind, it wasn't affecting his playing, thought Steve.

Hal just grinned.

The buzzer sounded. The next lines took over. At 9:12 Mel Hale powdered a ten-foot shot into the net to put the Chariots ahead, 4 to 2. Line Three kept up the hot scoring streak as right winger Ray VanSickle peppered in the fifth score.

As Line One returned to the ice for their last chance that second period, Steve expected some hard checking from the Angels, and got it. The clock read 5:19 when he stickhandled the puck across center ice, determined to sock in his third goal and earn himself a hat trick.

But Dick Wirtz seemed equally determined that Steve would not get what he wanted. Just over the blue line the Angels' center checked Steve with a hip blow that rocked the Chariots' center so hard his head swam. Not only did Steve lose control of the puck, but he lost his balance, too. He went down, hitting the ice and skidding across it for ten feet.

By the time Steve regained his balance, Dick had the puck and was stickhandling it toward center ice. Steve, struggling back to his feet, saw Mark and Hal skate after Dick. Both were fearless skaters. Steve was sure that if the entire line joined in an attack against them, neither would give an inch.

Dick made the mistake of trying to shoot the puck between them. Realizing what he intended to do, both players got in front of him like a human wall. The puck struck Mark's left skate and ricocheted toward the boards. At the same time Dick plowed into him and Hal, and it was only because Mark put his arms around Dick that none of them lost his balance and fell.

I'll never understand Mark as long as I keep playing with the Chariots, Steve thought. Even on the ice he doesn't forget that he's a gentleman.

An Angels' defenseman grabbed the puck off the boards and passed it to a teammate. During the next few moments of hard offensive playing, the Angels got the puck into Chariots' territory. And, as the clock ticked off 4:11, an Angels' defenseman found a target in the Chariots' net and hit it. Goalie Jason missed it by a mile.

Chariots 5, Angels 3.

None of the next two lines managed to score before the second period ended.

Steve was glad that there was only one more period to go. He was bushed. He removed his helmet and joined the rest of the team as it headed for the locker room. Again the coach, Kenneth Agard, Jr., came in with a pleased smile and a basketful of oranges.

"Gang, nice work!" he said proudly. "I knew you could do it! Here, an orange apiece. After the game we're going to stop at a restaurant for a real meal. Steak. How does that suit you?"

A shout of approval rose from the players.

It was while they were eating the oranges that Steve noticed one of the chaperones, Mr. Healy, was not in the room. He thought little about it until a few moments later when he looked around for Hal.

Hal wasn't in the room either.

Chapter 8

The third period started with Don Steuben, a sub, playing on Line One in place of Hal.

Where was Hal, anyway? Steve wondered, looking around and not seeing him. Was he sick? Or in trouble? From the way he'd been acting lately *something* was bothering him, Steve thought.

Then he saw Mr. Healy hurrying down the aisle, an anxious look on his stone-like face, and stopping to talk to Kenneth. They both looked excited, concerned. I bet it's about Hal, Steve thought. He's probably run away. Maybe that's what he wanted to see me about, to ask me if I'd run away with him.

The thought frightened Steve. He remembered the discussion he had with Mark about leaving the Chariots, leaving Kenneth, and getting the response that it was impossible. How do you like that? Steve thought as the impact of the situation hit him even harder. We really *are* Kenneth's prisoners, and can't do a thing about it! Not one thing! Who can blame Hal for running away?

Steve couldn't get the awful thought out of his mind, and twice during the first few moments he found himself bodychecked so hard that his legs were knocked from underneath him.

"C'mon, Steve!" Mark said to him. "Get with it!"

Gradually his concern, that he was one of Kenneth's unwilling players, was taken over by his natural abilities as a better-than-average hockey player, and in seconds he was back in the midst of all the action again. Three times he took shots at the goal, and all three times the Angels' goalie made a save. But Steve was in there fighting, and when the two minutes were up he was breathing tiredly and perspiring freely.

Fifteen seconds after Line Two took to the ice, Mel Hale was sent to the penalty box for high sticking, and for the next few seconds the Angels made a strong attempt to take advantage of the four-man team. A wild shot just missed the edge of the net and went flying against the boards. Jack Potter, the Chariots' red-headed, scrappy Line Two center, took the puck and "ragged" it for the next thirty-five seconds (ragging was keeping the puck to delay the game as long as possible). He stickhandled it down the side of the rink and across the ice, stopping abruptly to evade an Angel, then sprinting forward again, always in control of the puck. Chariot and Angel fans alike cheered as he craftily and successfully eluded his opponents.

At last Mel's penalty time was up; he returned to the ice. But the lines completed their two minutes without scoring.

It was when Line Three took the ice that Steve got a glimpse of Mr. Healy. The stone-faced chaperone was coming on the ice through the gate, pulling Hal Spoon after him. Hal, on his skates, seemed to be coming against his will. But he was coming.

"It doesn't pay to run away," said Mark, sitting next to Steve. "Nobody has ever gotten away with it yet. Hal will be sorry he tried it."

Steve stared at Mark. "Sorry?" he echoed. "Why should he be sorry? Is Kenneth going to hurt him, or something?"

Mark shrugged. For the first time, Mark didn't seem to have an answer.

Line Three failed to change the score, and Line One went back on the ice for the second time that period. Steve wondered if Hal would play, but Hal didn't. Kenneth, Steve saw, was having a "man-to-man" talk with him.

Mark's statement rang in Steve's ears even as the ref dropped the puck for the face-off. *It doesn't pay to run away. Nobody has ever gotten away with it yet.* That meant that others had tried it, too, and failed.

Steve played almost automatically during the two minutes, twice hearing Mark yelling at him, "Let's go, Steve! Let's go!"

He was sure that a combination of hard playing — and luck — was with the Chariots as they left the ice. They had failed to score, but they had kept the Angels from scoring, too.

It wasn't till Line Three's last time on the ice that another goal was made. Chariots' center Chuck Durling, carrying the puck across the Angels' blue line, seemed intent on going all the way. But, just as he neared the goal crease, he circled to the left. Drawing the anxious goalie after him, Chuck passed the puck to the wingman coming up behind him, Ray VanSickle. And Ray, taking advantage of the "deked" goalie (a move drawing the goalie out of position), shot the puck into the net.

Chariots 6, Angels 3.

A minute later the game was over, the Chariots receiving loud applause as they left the rink. One remark Steve heard from a fan was, "Never in my life have I seen a kids' team like those Chariots. They're fantastic!"

Steve had to agree. He knew he should feel proud of the win, and of his own performance. But the realization that he was a hockey "slave" of Kenneth Agard, Jr.'s, scared him. Whether the Chariots were Kenneth's "slaves," or "prisoners," or whatever name fitted, Steve couldn't believe that such a thing existed. How could it be allowed? he wondered. How could Kenneth, a kid no older than he was, get away with keeping guys on the team against their wishes? It was *crazy*.

But he *was* doing it. And he *was* getting away with it.

Steve shook.

At the restaurant, where Kenneth had made reservations, Steve told himself that he would never have eaten the steak, potatoes, and all that sumptuous-tasting salad if he weren't so ravenously hungry.

They stayed at a motel that night. The next morning they bused to the airport and took Flight 617 home. Steve was about to sit with Hal on the plane, when Mark told him that their seating arrangement was the same flying back as it was flying up. Disappointed, Steve rose and went to occupy the seat with Mark.

"I'm sorry, Steve," said Mark. "But it's the rules."

"Kenneth's rules, I suppose," Steve replied, disgruntled.

"He's boss," reminded Mark.

During most of the flight Steve was silent. Only once, out of curiosity, did he break the silence by asking Mark, "You never told me about your parents. What does *your* father do?"

Mark hesitated. "He's an invalid."

"Oh? I'm sorry."

"My mother's a secretary."

"Got any brothers and sisters?"

"One brother, two sisters. I came third."

"I'm the only child in my family," said Steve. "But I guess you know that."

They fell silent again. This time Steve wondered if that brief conversation had gotten Mark thinking about his family, too.

The next day Steve finally had a chance to tell Kenneth that he had had enough and wanted to go home. He found

87

Kenneth in his office, a large room whose walls were covered with book shelves and pictures — mostly hockey pictures. The head of the Chariots hockey team seemed lost behind a huge, oak desk on which were books, papers, pads, and a red telephone.

"Hey, nice game yesterday, Steve!" Kenneth exclaimed. He smiled as he leaned back in his swivel chair, put his elbows on its wide arms and steepled his fingers. "Played like a real pro."

"Thanks," Steve said, feeling good about the praise. "Did the best I could."

"No, you didn't. You could do better." Kenneth chuckled. "And that will come with experience — experience you'll gain the longer you're with us. I've got big plans for you, Steve. *Big* plans." He rocked a couple of times on the chair, then stopped and focused his eyes on Steve. "One of these days you're going to be rich. *Rich,* Steve. Hear me?"

"I don't want to be rich," Steve said,

meeting Kenneth's eyes directly. "I want out. Now."

The smile on Kenneth's face faded. A cold, hard look came over it as he glanced away from Steve's direct gaze and sat back in his chair. "You seem to have a short memory, Steve," he said calmly. "You can't get out. We've told you that."

Steve jumped to his feet. "Why not?" he shouted. "Who are you to keep me here a prisoner? I'll run away! I'll call the police!"

Kenneth's eyes turned back to Steve. For the first time since Steve had met Kenneth, Steve had never seen a look in the young co-owner's eyes as he was seeing now. It was the look of a leader — a tyrant — who knew what he wanted and got it, at whatever the cost.

"No, you won't," he said, his voice low, deliberate. "You're not going to do anything — but play hockey."

Steve sat back down, Kenneth's voice

hanging like a whip over him. He had once said to somebody — to Mark — that Kenneth was a monster. Now he was sure of it.

"Our discussion is over, Steve," Kenneth said, the cold glare gone from his eyes, his voice gentle — almost gentle — once again. "See you at breakfast."

Steve got up. "Yeah," he said, and left.

I can't believe this, he thought. What'll I do now?

A week later the Chariots flew to Buffalo for a game against the Blue Leafs. Steve, his mind made up that he wasn't going to stay with the Chariots no matter what Kenneth Agard, Jr., said, started at face-off with no desire to play. Hal was back after having been gone a few days, but Steve didn't know where he'd been, and Hal wasn't talking. He seemed raring to play, however.

The ref dropped the puck. The Blue Leafs' center, a kid with strong arms and chunky legs, grabbed the puck easily, and for the entire two-minute session the Chariots might as well have had only four men on the ice. At 16:42 the Blue Leafs scored.

If I don't play Kenneth will *have* to let me go, Steve thought.

When Line One got off the ice and Line Two got on it, Kenneth came and sat down beside Steve. If he was angry he didn't show it.

"Steve," he said, "you're not the first kid to act this way. Others have, and later changed their minds. You will be punished, naturally. Firstly, you'll have to skip a meal. Maybe two, or even three, depending on your cooperation. Secondly, you'll be dismissed of all the fun privileges: games, movies, and so on. Thirdly, a check won't go to your parents." He smiled at Steve. "Don't be a child all your life. Grow up. In mind, anyway."

He stood up. "Think about it," he said,

and returned to his seat near the gate.

Steve stared after him. A chill rippled up and then down his spine. He had never in his life met a kid like Kenneth Agard, Jr., he thought, and he hoped he never would again.

Line Two tied the score. Then Line Three broke it, only to have it tied again just seconds before they got off the ice.

Chariots 2, Blue Leafs 2.

As Line One started to leave the bench, Kenneth grabbed Steve by the arm. "I hope you gave it some thought, Steve," he said, smiling. "You're a very good athlete. I hope you're an intelligent one, too."

Steve looked directly into his eyes, but said nothing.

I have done a *lot* of thinking, Kenneth, he wanted to say. But I'm not going to tell you about what.

This time he grabbed the face-off and played as well — if not better — than in the game against the Angels. He was angry, and being angry made him more determined. He socked in a goal during the session, then assisted on another goal in the third session. The game turned out to be a scoring spree for the Chariots. It ended 9 to 3 in their favor. Steve was credited with a hat trick, having scored has third goal in the last period.

"Good game, Steve," Kenneth said, smiling, as the boys streamed off the ice. "I knew you were as intelligent as you were athletic."

Buttering me up, Steve thought. If he only knew what I have in mind.

Chapter 9

The players changed their clothes in the locker room, then were bused to their motel where Kenneth had reserved rooms for them for the night.

At seven o'clock they piled into the motel's dining room and had supper: duckling, mashed potatoes, and salad. A meal fit for a king, thought Steve. But — oh, man — wouldn't I go for a big, fat, juicy hamburger for a change!

Anyway, I still don't want a part of it. We're Kenneth's puppets. He pulls the strings and we jump, Steve reflected solemnly.

Another thing: How do we know that he really sends checks to our parents? We never see the checks. He could be lying. In any case, Mom and Dad lived without the checks before, and they could again.

Steve noticed that both Mr. Healy and Mr. Karpis were sitting near the head of the two tables. No one could possibly leave the room without at least one of the men seeing him.

The team's rooms were on the fourth floor, high enough, Steve realized, to discourage anybody from escaping.

Steve was in a room with three other boys, including Mark Slate. They watched TV till ten o'clock, then Mark clicked it off and turned off the light.

Steve lay in bed, his eyes open, his mind in high gear. He had decided that tonight he'd escape and go to the police — or make a bold attempt at it.

He glanced several times at his wrist watch. There was just enough light shining in through the drape-covered window to be able to read it. At a quarter of twelve he crawled out of bed, taking care not to wake any of the other guys. He dressed, picked up his shoes, and tiptoed to the door. Turning the knob, he opened the door carefully and peered out.

His heart sank as he saw one of the chaperones sitting on a chair down at the end of the hall. Man! Kenneth was really making sure that no one was going to run away!

Steve closed the door quietly and returned to the bed, his hopes of escaping gone down the drain. He lay on the covers for only a few minutes when he thought of the fire escape. Of course! Every motel at least three or four stories high had a fire escape!

He slid out of bed, tiptoed to the window, and peered out. There was a balcony, but no fire escape.

Once again his heart took a nose-dive. Couldn't he be just a bit lucky once?

Then he thought, wasn't there usually a fire escape from a balcony?

Excitement erased his hopeless feeling for a minute as he unlocked the window and groped for hand-grips to open it. He found them. Slowly, silently, he lifted the window, picked up his shoes, and crawled out.

He looked to the side of the balcony, and his heart jumped. There *was* a fire escape!

Quietly he closed the window, climbed over the balcony, stepped onto the fire escape, and started to make the swift, long descent to the dark alley below. A chill wind was blowing. By the time Steve reached the bottom his teeth were chattering.

Suddenly a voice above him cut through the night. "Steve! Come back here! You'll freeze to death in that cold!"

The voice was hard to recognize in the strong wind, and the face Steve saw peering over the balcony was just a shadowy blur. But he was sure it was Mark's.

Steve put his shoes on and ran. He reached the street and bolted to the right, the wind biting through his clothes. No one was on the street. There were no cars. The only lights were those on the high poles at the end of each block.

He crossed to the next block, ran on. Two men loomed out of the darkness ahead of him, and he turned and hid in the shadows of a building. When they went by he ran on, stumbled off the curb, and fell. He bruised his hands and dirtied his clothes, but he scrambled to his feet and raced on down the street.

Halfway down the block he saw what looked like a telephone booth. Hope flared in him as he sprinted toward it. It *was* a telephone booth! He entered it. His hands trembled as he took off the receiver.

But, how can I call the police? he

thought. I haven't got a cent on me! His throat ached.

He heard sharp heels clicking on the sidewalk, and he ducked. Was someone already after him? Had Mark gotten the message to Mr. Healy or Mr. Karpis so quickly that one of them could already be hot on his trail?

But the sound of the footsteps was not familiar. Nor did they have that hurrying sound that they would have if they belonged to someone chasing him.

Steve stood up, and saw a man coming briskly down the sidewalk. He was wearing a topcoat and hat, and had his coat collar turned up around his neck to protect it from the cold wind.

"Mister!" Steve cried, stepping out of the booth. "You got twenty cents I can have to make a phone call?"

The man stopped, startled, and peered at Steve hesitantly from under bushy eyebrows. He was old, Steve saw. In his fifties or sixties. And he was carrying a lunch pail. Probably going to work or going home from work, Steve figured.

He's hesitating because he thinks I'm a street bum, Steve thought. "Please, sir?" he said. "I really would like to make a phone call."

The man's gaze roved over Steve's hair, his clothes, his shoes. Sizing him up, like a man sizing up a car he's considering buying. "Kind of young to be out this late, aren't you?" he snorted. "And without a coat. You'll freeze your ears off."

"That's why I want to make the phone call, sir," Steve said, praying that the man would give him the money and not waste any more time.

"All right," the man said, pushing back his coat and taking out a coin purse. "And make sure you get home, okay? You're lucky I came around when I did."

"I know, sir," Steve said.

The man unzipped the coin purse,

picked out two dimes and handed them to Steve. "Here you are," he said.

"Thanks!" Steve cried, accepting the dimes. "I appreciate it, sir."

The man then stuck his coin purse back into his pocket, pulled his coat about him, gave Steve another quick, stern glance, then went on, his heels clicking on the sidewalk. I guess I can't blame him, Steve thought. I'd feel as he does, too, if I were in his place. Steve re-entered the phone booth, stuck the dimes into the proper slot, then dialed 0. The phone rang. Once . . . twice . . .

He looked up the street. Two men were coming from the direction of the motel! Mr. Healy and Mr. Karpis? Steve's heart pounded.

"Operator," said a calm voice over the receiver.

"Hello! Get me the police! Quick!" Steve cried.

"One moment, please."

Steve could hear the men's feet

101

pounding on the pavement. In a moment they would be crossing the intersection.

"Sergeant Williams speaking," a man's deep voice said into his ear. "Can I help you?"

"Yes!" Steve said. "This is Steve Crandall! I'm with the Chariots hockey team, and I'm . . . I'm in deep trouble!"

"Now take it easy," Sergeant Williams's voice came calmly over the wire. "Just what kind of deep trouble —"

Steve couldn't take another second to explain what kind of trouble he was in. The two men — Mr. Healy and Mr. Karpis — were running across the intersection and would catch him in no time if he didn't hightail it out of there. He dropped the phone and, wrenched with fear, sprinted out of the telephone booth. What would the men do to him if they caught him? Take him back to the motel? Beat him up?

He raced to the end of the block, and

was halfway down the next one when one of the men caught up to him and grabbed him by the arm.

"Okay, kid," said Mr. Healy, his breath coming in gasps. "That's enough. Kenneth won't like this one bit. Not one bit."

He started to drag Steve back to the motel and met Mr. Karpis who had just emerged from the telephone booth. Steve's heart sank. Now they knew who he was trying to call!

"Did you find out who he was calling?" Mr. Healy asked.

"No. I just got some operator," Mr. Karpis grunted.

Steve started to breathe a sigh of relief when Mr. Healy grabbed him by the collar. "Did you talk to a cop?" he snapped, glaring at him.

"No! I was trying to get my parents . . . but I didn't have time," Steve answered.

"You'd better be telling the truth, kid," said Healy, and for a moment Steve thought Healy would swat him across the face, but he only grabbed Steve by a wrist and started pulling him down the street, back to the motel. They headed quickly for the elevator before the clerk, sitting at a desk inside a small office, could notice them. They rode up to the fourth floor where Mr. Karpis stopped at Room 431, unlocked the door, and went in. Mr. Healy escorted Steve to Room 433.

"You'll stay in here with me till morning," Mr. Healy commanded, closing the door behind them. His eyes were like hot coals as he looked down at Steve. "I've never beat up a kid, but getting me out in this kind of night sure makes me want to do it to you."

Steve cringed. He was sure Mr. Healy would do it, too. Both he and Mr. Karpis acted like two different men when they had caught him on the street . . . almost like hardened criminals who wouldn't hesitate a second to hurt him.

Mr. Healy shoved Steve toward one of the single beds. "Get out of your clothes and into bed," he ordered. "And hurry. Running away is bad enough without your getting sick, too."

Shivering from a combination of cold and fear, Steve kicked off his shoes, pulled off his clothes, and crawled under the covers. He was angry, but more angry at himself for failing to escape than from what to expect from Kenneth Agard, Jr.

Chapter 10

Steve ignored Mark at breakfast and during the entire flight back home, blaming Mark for having "squealed" on him to the two chaperones.

"I'm sorry, Steve," Mark said apologetically. "But I had to do it. Kenneth depends on me. You shouldn't have run away."

Oh, sure, Steve wanted to say, anger steaming up inside him. But he kept silent.

For some reason of his own, Kenneth didn't talk with Steve about Steve's running away until after they were settled back at his home. There, two hours later, Mark came after Steve in the Recreation Room.

"Steve, Kenneth wants to see you," he said.

Silently, Steve followed him out of the room to Kenneth's den. The young mentor of the Chariots hockey team was ensconced in his swivel chair behind the huge, oak desk.

"Hello, Steve," he greeted him pleasantly. "Please sit down."

Steve sat on a plush armchair at the opposite side of the desk. Kenneth nodded to Mark, and Mark left.

"Steve," Kenneth began, picking up a folded sheet of printed matter, "you've seen this before. Remember it?"

Steve's eyes widened. He nodded. "It's the contract you asked me to sign. But I never did."

"Look again, Steve," said Kenneth, pointing at a signature on the second page.

Steve leaned forward, and a rush of

108

anger swept over him. There, on the dotted line, was his name in his own handwriting! And below it, his father's!

"I didn't sign that!" he cried. "And neither did my Dad! Someone forged those signatures!"

Kenneth smiled. "Say what you want to, but it's your signature and your father's, and they bind you to me and to the Chariots. So, no matter what you do, Steve, you will only be hurting yourself. And, of course, the team."

"I don't want to play with you anymore," Steve said flatly. "I want to go home."

"You can't," said Kenneth. "You have an obligation, and you can't back out of it. It's only a waste of time and energy, believe me. You're not the only one who felt misused, or disenchanted, during the first two or three weeks. Others have, too, and tried to run away. Oh, not many. Hal Spoon, as you know. And a couple of others. It took them a while to realize how really childish they were."

He lay the contract back on the desk, got up, and went to the door. "Of course, you'll have to be penalized, Steve," he went on in that same, unruffled tone. "I'm sorry. But I have made strict regulations here, and I must see that everybody abides by them. You'll be under Mr. Healy's attention for the next couple of days."

Mr. Healy was outside of the door, waiting for Steve. He took Steve's arm and led him down the hall to another room. He switched on a light, told Steve to read the instructions that were tacked on the door, and left. Steve tried to turn the knob, but couldn't. He was locked in.

He read the instructions.

1. This will be your quarters for the next 48 hours.
2. Your meal will be brought in to you three times a day.
3. As you see, there is no television for you to watch, no book to read, no paper, or pencil with which to write. You will

have nothing to do, although any exercise you do would be to your advantage.
4. There is a button on the desk. Press
it if you want any help.

A lump formed in Steve's throat as
he looked around him. There was a bed,
a chair, a lamp, a desk, and a rectan-
gular mirror hung on one wall. Above
the mirror was a round, framed object
that looked like a built-in speaker. A
door was open, showing a small room
with a toilet and sink inside.

I can't believe it! Steve thought. This
room is a jail cell! I'm in solitary confinement!

His heart pounding, Steve stepped to
the desk and pressed the button that
was on the right-hand side of it.

A moment later Kenneth's voice answered through the speaker. "What is
it, Steve?"

*What is it, Steve? You would think
that everything was hunky-dory!*

"I want to get out of here, that's what!" Steve yelled. "You can't keep me in here!"

"You'll be in there for forty-eight hours, Steve," Kenneth said, not a ruffle in his voice. "Try to do some exercise, and then rest. You might even sleep. You'll find that time goes fastest that way."

"Kenneth, you're a monster!" cried Steve, glaring at the speaker.

He received no reply.

"You hear me? You're a monster!" he shouted, then jumped onto the bed, holding back tears that fought to come.

What could he do? Nothing. He was Kenneth's prisoner.

He got his first meal in half an hour. It was a bowl of cereal, a banana, and a glass of milk. There was nothing wrong with that, he admitted.

He was worried about what his noon lunch, and his dinner, would be. Would he be given the same meal as he had for breakfast?

112

Surprisingly, the lunch he received was of the same high quality as the meals that were served to the team. It was the same with dinner. He had to admit that the meals were more than satisfactory.

But the loneliness of the almost bare room, and the quietness of it, got to him. The only sounds he heard were his own breathing, his footsteps when he walked across the bare floor, and the protesting springs when he lay on the bed. Not a sound came from outside of the room.

That night, as he thought of his mother and father, he wept. Did they really know where he was? he wondered. Did they know that he played with the Chariots? Or had Kenneth really talked with them and gotten their permission to let Steve play hockey with the Chariots? Or had Kenneth lied about the whole thing?

Two days later Kenneth's voice sounded warm and pleasant as it came over the speaker. "Good morning, Steve.

113

I trust you had a good night's sleep."

Steve, sitting on the edge of the bed in his pajamas — at least Kenneth was generous enough to give him those, too — nodded. "I did," he said.

"Good. Can I have your word that you won't pull anything foolish again? "

Steve hesitated.

"Okay. You need not answer that," said Kenneth. "You know what the consequences are, except that the next time your confinement would be for three days. Mr. Healy will be there in a minute to take you to breakfast. Meanwhile, I won't see you till hockey practice this afternoon. You're a good protégé, Steve. Listen to me, and you won't ever be sorry."

Steve told himself that he would never again want to spend time in that cell-like room. But he wasn't going to stay with the Chariots, either.

Somehow he was going to find a way to get away from them, and from the clutches of Kenneth Agard, Jr.

Chapter 11

Steve almost cried out with joy when he heard that the Chariots were going to Mulberry City on Saturday to play the Condors. Mulberry City, situated on a lake about one hundred miles north of Water Falls, was where his Uncle Mike lived.

Wouldn't it be great if Uncle Mike read about the Chariots and went to the game? But Steve knew that he might as well wish for a trip to the moon: Uncle Mike didn't give a hoot for hockey.

The team bused to Mulberry City.

Even though Mark and Steve sat together, not a word was mentioned about Steve's solitary confinement. Nor did Steve mention a word to Mark about his Uncle Mike's living in Mulberry City.

Maybe — just maybe — I might find a chance to telephone Uncle Mike, Steve thought hopefully.

There was something else about Mulberry City that bolstered his hopes. It had a college with a fine hockey team, and a kid's hockey league that had been spawning a state championship team for the last three years.

A couple of times in the past Steve's mother and father had brought him there to see a game. Wouldn't it be something, he thought, if they came to see this one? Or would Kenneth have informed them about it?

I doubt it, Steve thought. I can't see him letting our parents know about a game every time the Chariots play near their hometown.

Arriving in Mulberry City, the Chariots rode directly to the rink, passing beneath banners that were strung across the streets:

CONDORS vs CHARIOTS
DEC. 2

When the team entered the rink Steve could see that the promotion had really paid off: half of the stadium was already filled, and people were still pouring in.

Playing opposite Steve at center was a boy named Curt Hilliard. He was shorter than Steve, but more powerful around the shoulders. He was also aggressive, as Steve discovered when the ref dropped the puck and blew the face-off whistle.

Curt moved like a dart, taking the puck and passing it quickly to a wingman. The fine play drew a loud cheer for the black-uniformed Condors' center, and a few scattered boos for Steve.

117

"A little slow, weren't you?" a fan needled him.

Forgetting how he had felt before the game, Steve was suddenly determined that he wasn't going to let Curt get away with it. He hightailed it toward the Chariots' net with flecks of ice spurting up from his skates like tiny chips, zipped past Hal and Nick, and got to the puck carrier. Reaching out his stick, Steve rammed into the Condor with a hip-jarring check that knocked the player off balance. He grabbed the puck, circled and started to head back toward center ice when Curt almost met Steve head-on. With a snap of his stick, Steve passed the disk to Mark.

Almost at the same instant Curt hit him, then stayed glued to him as they glided across the ice till they crashed against the boards.

"So you're one of those great Chariot players, are you?" Curt said to him just before they broke apart. "Well, we'll see."

118

Both of them sprinted up the ice, crossing the neutral zone into Condors' territory where Mark had just passed the puck to Nick. Nick stickhandled the puck along the side of the ice, then passed it to Hal. Just as Hal received it, a Condor defenseman checked him, making him lose control of the puck. The other defenseman skated up, grabbed the puck, and started to carry it back toward center ice.

Noticing Curt in between him and the defenseman, Steve could see the next move coming. Putting on a burst of speed he got in front of Curt at almost the same instant that the defenseman passed the puck. Steve reached out his stick, hooked the puck and started to swerve out of Curt's path with it when he felt something — the blade of a stick — hook around his ankle. He fell and slid across the ice on his knees, as the whistle shrilled.

He looked around and saw the ref

119

skating toward the timekeeper's bench, holding up a finger and shouting, "Tripping! Number Two!"

A moment later, Curt, his head bowed in disgust, was skating slowly toward the penalty box.

He wasn't in there long, however, for Line One's time on the ice was soon up.

"Nice play, Steve," Mark said as they headed through the gate to sit down and rest. "Especially against that hothead."

"He's good, though," Steve admitted.

By now he was sure that neither his Uncle Mike nor his mother and father were at the game. He would have heard them if they were.

At 14:36 Mel Hale socked one into the net for the Chariots' first goal.

"It's our turn," said Mark as Line One returned to the ice for the second time.

In the face-off circle Curt's eyes locked with Steve's. Vengeance lurked in their brown, shining depths. Then both centers turned their attention to the spot between them, tension building up as they waited for the ref's whistle.

Shreeek! The puck dropped. This time the sticks struck at the disk simultaneously, and Steve could feel his opponent's strength in his stick. I wonder how many sticks he's broken so far this year? Steve thought, not too amused.

But Curt's stick didn't break as he won the scramble and passed the puck to a wingman. Again cheers rose from the fans for Curt, and boos for Steve. But the Chariots' center took the calls in stride now. He just had to play harder the next time, he reflected.

At 11:02 Curt, taking a long pass from one of his wingmen, took two steps toward the Chariots' net and sent the puck flying past Jason Moore's right knee for a goal. Chariots 1, Condors 1.

A smirk lingered on Curt's face as he looked at Steve in the face-off circle. "One up on you," he said, boasting.

121

"I know," said Steve.

The puck dropped and the whistle blew. Steve's stick flashed. It struck the puck a fraction of a second before Curt's did and zipped across the ice toward Nick. Steve moved at the same time, sprinting past Curt and over the Condors' blue line in a straight path for the net.

A Condors' defenseman checked Nick, then pokechecked the puck in an effort to grab it. The disk spun away, got up on edge for a second, and rolled. Steve went after it. In a sweeping glide he yanked it toward him with the blade of his stick. In the same continuous motion he shot the puck toward the net.

Like a small, black flying saucer it raised off the ice and flew through the air past the goalie's masked face for a goal. Chariots 2, Condors 1.

Sticks from the Chariots' bench clattered against the boards, drowning out the few cheers that sprang from the fans.

Steve, doubtful that they were Chariots' cheers, suspected that they came out of respect for his fine shot.

A grin flickered on his face as he stood in the face-off circle. "We're even," he said to Curt.

"Yeah," Curt mumbled.

A Condors' wingman tied the score with a slap shot seconds before the two minutes were up, and the lines relinquished the ice to Lines Two. Chariots 2, Condors 2.

It wasn't till Line Three got on the ice, though, that the 2 to 2 tie was broken. The Chariots' left defenseman Jerry McMann scored the goal with an assist from left winger Abe Nolan.

The third session went by scoreless. The Chariots led, 3 to 2.

No sooner had the teams skated to their locker rooms for their ten-minute intermission than the thought struck Steve again: I must get to a telephone and call Uncle Mike sometime during, or after, this game. He's got to come and help me get away from Kenneth and his odd-ball cohorts.

But how? he thought. I failed once. How can I expect to get away without getting caught again this time?

Chapter 12

Steve rested his head back against the door of a locker and closed his eyes. He was tired. But the main reason for his closing his eyes was to think, and to discourage anybody from talking to him.

Could he make the break as the teams started back on the ice? he wondered. Should he wait until the second intermission when the chaperones might not be as cautious? Or should he wait until after the game? He had to do it *sometime*.

I'll wait till the second intermission,

he decided. It's possible that we won't be as closely watched then. And I'll just play hockey as if nothing else in the world could be more important.

At face-off, as the second period started, Curt Hilliard looked up and stared at Steve almost in a daze as the Chariots' center grabbed the puck. Stickhandling it along the red line toward the boards in front of the Condors' bench, Steve controlled the puck as if it were an extension of his stick.

A Condors' wingman was almost upon him before he passed it to Mark. Mark took it across the blue line and passed it to Nick. At the same time Steve bolted down the middle of the ice. Nick spotted him and shot him a pass, then sped on toward the net.

Steve grabbed the puck just as a Condors' defenseman checked him. For a moment lights flashed before his eyes like lightning bugs and he lost sight of the puck. Whirling, he felt and heard

126

the collision of metal as his right skate crashed into another. A player in a black uniform spun and hit the ice.

Then Steve heard the familiar crack of stick meeting puck. He looked around and saw the black disk skimming over the ice into Chariots' territory and past the goal.

Shreeek! went the whistle.

"Icing!" the ref called.

He skated to the puck, scooped it up, and brought it back to the right-hand circle near the Condors' net for a face-off.

Steve and a Condors' defenseman faced off. Once again Steve grabbed the puck and shot it to Mark. Mark stopped it and smashed it toward the net, but a Condors' man deflected it, getting tangled with Hal Spoon as he did so.

Nick rushed in. His stick flashed.

Crack! The puck blazed past the goalie's left foot into the net. It was 4 to 2, Chariots.

Three seconds after the face-off the lines' two minutes were up.

The next two sessions went by scoreless. Steve, his legs aching in spite of the four-minute rest he had taken while the second and third lines were on the ice, was glad the period had ended.

He hadn't forgotten about his plan, either. Just seconds before the clock had run out he had untied the laces of his skates. It would take only a matter of seconds to slip them off.

Keeping in the middle of the crowd as it funneled out of the gate toward the locker rooms, Steve saw the chaperones, Mr. Healy and Mr. Karpis, standing just outside of the Chariots' locker-room door. It was to the left of the gate; the Condors' was to the right.

Great! thought Steve, as if the world had collapsed on him. The entrance to the rink is to the left! I can't possibly get out of here without their seeing me!

Then a second breath of hope filled

128

his heart. There, at the bottom of the balcony to his right, was a blazing red sign: EXIT.

Ducking and mixing in with the Condors' players, he headed for the exit. As the players began to swarm into their locker room, Steve removed his skates, straightened up, and bolted down the aisle.

He dropped the skates to the side and rushed around a corner to a door. For a moment his heart seemed to hang in limbo as the fear hit him that the door might be locked.

He tried it. It wasn't. He pulled it open and plunged out into the cold afternoon air.

He raced across the sidewalk and the packed parking lot, then down the street, looking hopefully for a store or telephone booth. There was neither one in sight.

He reached the end of the block, panting from the hard run, and glanced down at his socks; they were coming loose. But he couldn't take the time to remove them now. Every second was a precious gem that could lead him to help and complete safety. It could be his final chance to get away from Kenneth Agard, Jr., for good.

He took a moment to glance behind him, and almost froze.

Coming after him at a fast run was Mr. Healy!

Oh, no! thought Steve, and hurried on. He came to an alley, cut through it, then down a flight of steps that led to a backyard. At the bottom step he stubbed his big toe and fell flat on his stomach. Scrambling to his feet, he started ahead again. But he had gone only about ten feet when strong fingers locked around his arm.

As if this time the world had really collapsed on him, Steve looked around at the dark, icy stare of Mr. Healy.

"I guess I'll have to teach you one

way or another that you can't run away," the chaperone said, and raised his right hand.

Steve shut his eyes tight and winced as he waited for Mr. Healy to hit him.

"Hold it right there!" a voice said sharply. "Strike him and I'll make mince meat out of you!"

Steve's eyes shot open. That voice! He hadn't heard it in a long time, but he'd recognize it anywhere!

"Dad!" he cried.

Then he saw his mother, and another man — a tall, dark-haired, gentle-faced man — standing next to his father. "Mom! Uncle Mike!"

Tears glistened in his eyes as he rushed into their arms. When he regained his composure, and knew for sure that this time he was really safe, he said happily, "I didn't think I'd ever see any of you again."

"It was your phone call from Buffalo that started our investigation," Mr.

Crandall explained as they headed back for the rink. Ahead of them were Mr. Healy and a tall, slim man whom Steve had been introduced to a few minutes ago: Mr. Jason Williams, an FBI man. "The policeman who answered your call did some other calling and finally traced your name back to us. That took a lot of time. It wasn't till a couple of days ago that we found out you played with the Chariots hockey team and that the team was going to play here in Mulberry City."

Steve stared at him. "You didn't know till *just a couple of days ago?*"

"That's right," said his mother, her hazel eyes brimming with warmth now. "We've had the police looking for you since the night you disappeared."

"Well, we had to wait twenty-four hours before the police could put you on the missing persons list," Mr. Crandall explained. "But, that's right. That's how long we've been searching for you."

"I can't believe it!" Steve exclaimed.

"Well, you and all the players for the Chariots were playing under an assumed name," Uncle Mike joined in. "That's what made it so tough for the police and the FBI."

"But Kenneth Agard, Jr., said that we had signed papers," Steve said to his father. "And that you'd be getting a check every month."

"Hogwash," Mr. Crandall snorted. "He had lied all the way through. He's just as corrupt as his father, Kenneth Agard, Sr. They both gambled on a hockey team made up of fine young athletes in hopes of brainwashing them of everything except their desire to play hockey. When the kids reached sixteen they were to be placed with a higher age grouped team for further seasoning before joining Mr. Agard, Sr.'s, professional team. Mr. Agard, Sr., confessed everything."

"They picked on kids who were excellent skaters, and whose parents could use more money," said Uncle Mike. "But," he added, his eyes twinkling, "they didn't count on a kid loaded with spunk like you."

Steve smiled. "Thanks, Uncle Mike. But what about the other kids? What's going to happen to them?"

"They'll be taken home, of course," answered his mother.

"What about Kenneth, Jr.?" Steve asked. "He's the real brains behind the Chariots hockey team."

"Oh, he'll be taken care of properly, all right," his father said. "He's under age to be punished like an adult, but you can bet your boots he's going to pay for what he's done. The FBI doesn't cater to people who are in the business of kidnapping and forging contracts for illegal purposes."

"Where is he now?" Steve asked. "Has he been arrested yet?"

Mr. Crandall smiled. "Speak of the devil . . . look to your left," he said.

135

Steve did, and saw Kenneth Agard, Jr., being escorted toward a squad car by two policemen. Suddenly the young coach of the Chariots hockey team paused in his tracks and looked at Steve. For a moment Steve thought that Kenneth was going to say something to him, but he didn't. He turned away, squared his shoulders, and continued to the squad car.

I feel sorry for him, Steve thought. He's got brains. He could have used them to better advantage.

Then he saw Mark Slate coming out of the exit with several of the other players and a tall, square-shouldered man Steve assumed was also an FBI agent. Mark paused for a second, saw Steve, and said something to the man. The man nodded, and Mark turned and came walking toward Steve. He stopped a couple of feet in front of Steve, looking pale and ashamed.

"I'm sorry, Steve," he said. "I guess

136

it took this to make me realize how wrong it all was. I hope you won't hate me."

"I can't hate you, Mark," Steve said. "In spite of everything, you're still my friend. What are you going to do?"

"Go home," said Mark. "I miss my parents, too, and the rest of my family."

Steve put out his hand. Mark took it. "Good-bye, Steve," he said.

"Good-bye, Mark," said Steve.

Mark turned, and left.

Steve looked at his mother, father, and Uncle Mike, took a deep breath, and sighed.

"Know what I'd like to have right now?" he said, feeling the best that he had felt in a long, long time.

"What?" His mother's eyes were wide, expectant, as if to say anything he asked for he could have.

"A big, fat, juicy hamburger!" he exclaimed.

How many of these Matt Christopher sports classics have you read?

❑ Baseball Flyhawk
❑ Baseball Pals
❑ The Basket Counts
❑ Catch That Pass!
❑ Catcher with a Glass Arm
❑ Challenge at Second Base
❑ The Comeback Challenge
❑ The Counterfeit Tackle
❑ The Diamond Champs
❑ Dirt Bike Racer
❑ Dirt Bike Runaway
❑ Face-Off
❑ Football Fugitive
❑ The Fox Steals Home
❑ The Great
   Quarterback Switch
❑ Hard Drive to Short
❑ The Hockey Machine
❑ Ice Magic
❑ Johnny Long Legs
❑ The Kid Who Only
   Hit Homers
❑ Little Lefty
❑ Long Shot for Paul
❑ Long Stretch at First Base

❑ Look Who's Playing
   First Base
❑ Miracle at the Plate
❑ No Arm in Left Field
❑ Pressure Play
❑ Red-Hot Hightops
❑ Return of the
   Home Run Kid
❑ Run, Billy, Run
❑ Shoot for the Hoop
❑ Shortstop from Tokyo
❑ Skateboard Tough
❑ Soccer Halfback
❑ The Submarine Pitch
❑ Supercharged Infield
❑ Tackle Without a Team
❑ Tight End
❑ Too Hot to Handle
❑ Top Wing
❑ Touchdown for Tommy
❑ Tough to Tackle
❑ Undercover Tailback
❑ Wingman on Ice
❑ The Year Mom Won
   the Pennant

All available in paperback from Little, Brown and Company

Face-Off

Face-Off

by Matt Christopher

illustrated by Harvey Kidder

Little, Brown and Company
BOSTON   NEW YORK   TORONTO   LONDON

First Paperback Edition

Library of Congress Catalog Card No. 78-189258

ISBN 0-316-13994-7

20   19   18   17   16   15   14   13   12   11

MV NY

Published simultaneously in Canada
by Little, Brown & Company (Canada) Limited

Printed in the United States of America

To the McEligots,
Lee, John, Jack, Sue,
Michael, Mark and Michelle

Face-Off

1

"WATCH OUT for the falls!"

The yell came from one of the two boys standing on the bank beside the frozen pond.

Scott Harrison, skating past a marker — one of two large rocks placed about twenty feet apart on the ice — glanced at the edge of the pond some thirty feet away, and heard the roar of the falls in the clear, silent air. He grinned. No chance!

He turned as sharply as he could around the marker, noticing that Pete

Sewell, the kid he was racing, had just reached his marker. And he had given Pete a twenty-foot handicap, too!

Scott sped down the pond and reached the spot on the ice opposite Cathy, his younger sister, who was refereeing the race.

"The winner!" Cathy yelled, lifting her hands and jumping up on the toes of her skates.

Scott jumped and spun in midair, landing on one skate. He saw Pete cross the invisible line about five feet away and grinned.

"Well," said Pete, skating up to where Scott had stopped beside Cathy, "you did it again."

"You just won't give up, will you, Pete?" Cathy laughed.

Pete's blue eyes twinkled. "One of these days!" he said.

Scott remembered the warning cry from one of the boys on the bank and looked up there. They were sitting on a bench and putting on skates. Even at this distance Scott could see that the skates were the tube kind used in hockey.

"Who are those guys, Scott?" asked Pete.

"I don't know, but they go to our school," said Scott.

"The shorter one is Del Stockton," said Cathy. "I've heard Bev talk about him."

Bev was Judy Kerpa's sister, and Judy was Cathy's friend.

"Who's the tall, skinny kid?" asked Scott.

"I don't know."

Scott dug the toe of his right skate into the ice and skated off toward the center, whipping first to the left and then swinging in a circle around to the right and back again in a beautiful figure eight.

"Hey, Scott! Wait a minute!"

Scott pulled up short and saw the two boys skating toward him. The shorter one, Del Stockton, waved.

They pulled up in front of Scott, ice chips flying as they came to a quick stop. "Hi!" said the shorter of the two. "I'm Del Stockton and this is Skinny McCay. I've seen you at our school."

"I've seen you, too," said Scott, wondering how they knew his name.

"Mind racing with me?"

Scott looked at him in surprise. Del was his height and a few pounds lighter. "Why?"

Del grinned and shrugged. His cheeks were pink from the cold. "Okay. Forget it."

He started to sprint away when Cathy piped up, "Race with him, Scott."

6

Del must have heard her, for he quickly stopped and headed back toward them, skating backwards. He was fast, Scott saw, as fast skating backwards as some kids were skating frontwards. Scott glared at Cathy, thinking, *You had to open your big mouth.*

"We're not betting money," explained Del. "It's just for fun."

"Go ahead, Scott," urged Cathy. "If there's no bet, what're you afraid of?"

Scott shot another glaring look at her. One thing about Cathy: for a young squirt she wasn't afraid to say what she thought. Nor, sometimes, did she care whom she embarrassed. Like now.

"Aw, Del," Skinny McCay spoke up for the first time. "He's bashful. Let him alone."

"Yeah, okay." Del grinned again. "Forget it, Scott. I shouldn't have asked."

He started away again, but hadn't gone more than a yard when Scott stopped him. "Okay. I'll race with you."

"Good!" Del swung around in a half-circle and came to a quick stop in front of Scott. "You pick out the starting point and the finish line."

"Down here," Cathy said, and led the group a short distance down the ice to the spot where Scott had started his race with Pete Sewell. It was between two trees that stood opposite each other on the banks flanking the pond.

"Down around those two rocks and back," said Del. "Okay?"

"Okay," echoed Scott. "Give us the count, Cath."

The boys stood in line and crouched, ready to go.

"One! Two! Three! Go!" yelled Cathy, and the boys took off, their skates biting into the ice as they sprinted toward the

rocks about eighty yards away. *Phut!*
Phut! Phut! It was a language only ice
skates could speak.

They were even most of the way. Then
Scott pulled ahead. He stayed ahead as he
reached the rock on the right-hand side
and skated sharply around it, keeping his
turning circle less than five feet beyond
the rock. Heading back on the return trip
to the finish line he glanced at Del Stockton and saw the boy make the turn
even more sharply around the rock on
the left-hand side.

Del had gained a few feet on Scott as
he came around the turn, but Scott remained in the lead by about four feet. Del
stepped up his pace, his arms swinging
back and forth as he tried to close the gap
between him and Scott.

"Come on, Scott! Come on!" yelled
Cathy.

Scott put on more speed. He crossed

the finish line and knew he had won, even if Cathy hadn't jumped and shouted as she did. "You won, Scott! You won!"

He slowed up and glided around to meet Del coming toward him. They stopped and Del stuck out his hand, smiling. "I guess I should have kept my mouth shut," he said. "You're really a fast skater."

"Thanks," said Scott.

"Can you skate backwards?"

"Hardly."

"You ought to practice it," suggested Del.

Scott noticed Del's skates, and also Skinny McCay's. "They're hockey skates, aren't they?" he asked.

"Right," said Del. "Ever play hockey?"

"Never."

"Be at Cass Rink tonight at six-thirty," said Skinny. "We play with the Golden Bears in the Bantam Hockey League. If you want to play, maybe Coach Roberts will put you on one of the lines."

Scott had thought about playing hockey, but had never had the nerve to go out for it.

"You think he would?" he asked, trying not to show how pleased he was at the prospect of playing.

"You're a lot faster skater than most of the guys we've got," said Del. "He should."

"We'll be the Three Icekateers," smiled Skinny.

For a long minute Scott stood there, moving back and forth on his skates. Cathy and Pete were jabbering about something, but he didn't hear a word they said.

2

THERE'S ONE CATCH," said Del. "If you play you'll have to get your own stick and skates. Those won't do." He pointed at the flat-bottomed skates Scott was wearing.

"You can get your stuff at Fred's Sporting Goods," drawled Skinny. "Tell 'em you're playing with us and they'll give you a discount."

Scott thought of the mailbox bank in his room where he put his allowance each week and whatever money he earned from shoveling neighbors' sidewalks and driveways. He figured he must have be-

13

tween eight to twelve dollars, hardly enough to buy a hockey stick and skates.

He looked at his wristwatch and saw that it was close to five-thirty. Mom would have supper ready in fifteen to twenty minutes. Six-thirty would come before he knew it.

"C'mon, Cath," he said, "We'd better get home. So long, Del . . . Skinny! Glad to have met you!"

"Same here!" they called back to him.

Scott and Cathy skated to the bench, took off their skates, and put on their shoes. Pete went along with them. He lived next door. Because he had no brother or sister he usually trailed after either Scott and Cathy or one of the other neighbors.

They walked home, their skates strung over their shoulders. It was a ten-minute walk to Chippewa, the Indian name given

14

to their street. The name of the town was Shattuck. Scott and Cathy had lived here all their lives.

Pete said good-bye and walked up the snow-packed driveway leading to his home. As Scott and Cathy walked up their own driveway they saw a light in the garage and figured that Dad was tinkering with the car again.

"Hi, Dad!" shouted Scott.

"Hello!" came Dad's voice from inside the garage. As the children headed for the kitchen door they saw Dad crouched over the right front fender, his head hidden behind the upraised hood of the car.

"Tell Mother I'll be in for supper in two shakes!" he yelled to them.

Scott smelled something good cooking the moment he opened the door. "Chicken and dumplings!" he cried. "Man! Will I go for that!"

15

"Was wondering how soon you'd be home," said Mom, coming in from the dining room, where she had just set the table. She looked like a young girl with her dark hair cut in bangs and her figure trim. "Hurry. Supper's about ready."

Both Scott and Cathy were finished washing when Dad came in. He tossed his coat over a chair, then washed his greasy hands. He was all of six feet tall, broad-shouldered and muscular. His stomach bulged a little bit, though, a condition Mom — and sometimes the children — kidded him about.

They sat at the table and said in unison, "Bless this food and us, O Lord, and thank you for the gifts you have given us this day. Amen."

"And please help me get on the Golden Bears hockey team," added Scott.

Three pairs of eyes focused on him. "What was that?" asked Dad.

16

"He's going to play hockey with the Golden Bears!" Cathy cried before Scott had a chance to answer.

"Wait a minute, will you?" snapped Scott. "Nobody is *sure* I am."

"All right," said Mom. "Back off, both of you, and let's hear it from the beginning — from Scott."

Scott sighed. "Well," he began, and told it from the beginning, except that there wasn't much to tell and he had to leave soon to be at Cass Rink by six-thirty.

"So you have to furnish a hockey stick and skates yourself," said Dad.

"I haven't checked my bank yet," said Scott, "but I don't think I've enough to buy both. I'm going to ask Buck Weaver if I can sell papers for him for a week. I know he'll let me. He hates his paper route in the wintertime."

He arrived at Cass Rink a few minutes before six-thirty. It was crowded with

17

kids, and so noisy you couldn't hear yourself think. All except three boys wore regular clothes, with sweaters or jackets. Each had on a helmet and each had a hockey stick and wore skates. The three boys, Scott was sure, were goalies from the looks of their heavy, padded uniforms, extra-large sticks and shin guards.

"There he is!" a voice shouted above the din. "Hey, Scott!"

Skinny McCay broke from the crowd and sprinted toward him. Del trailed. He didn't seem as excited about seeing Scott as Skinny did.

"Hi," greeted Scott. He felt jittery, scared. "Everybody's got a stick," he said. "And a helmet."

"Don't worry," drawled Skinny. "Coach Roberts will get you a stick and a helmet even if he has to take it from somebody."

Scott smiled. If Skinny skated as slowly

as he talked he would be next to useless!

"C'mon," said Skinny. "We'll introduce you to Coach Roberts."

We? Del didn't seem to care whether he went along or not.

Scott saw a man surrounded by several kids near the goal netting and followed Skinny to him.

"Coach Roberts!" cried Skinny.

The coach looked up. He was tall and thin and wore a blue turtleneck sweater. "Hi, Skinny."

Skinny skated up to him with Scott close behind. "This is the kid I was telling you about, Coach. Scott Harrison."

The coach smiled and put out his hand. Scott gripped it. "Hi, Scott. Heard you beat Del Stockton in a race."

Scott shrugged shyly.

"Ever play hockey?"

"Just shinny," said Scott.

19

"Then you've got some learning to do. But don't worry. It won't take you long — not if you're fast on your skates." He glanced at Scott's skates. "You'll have to get hockey skates. But I'll let you get away with those today. Don't you have a stick?"

"No."

The coach looked at a stocky boy beside him. "Fat, there are a couple on a bench in the locker room. Bring one, will you, please?"

Fat squirted away.

Skinny nudged Scott. "Fat's my brother," he said. "You wouldn't believe it, but he plays center. So do I."

"When you buy your hockey stick, hold it in your hands and test it for its length, weight and lie," said Coach Roberts. "The lie is the angle the blade makes with the shaft. You will also have to get a helmet and a mouth guard. We'll furnish the rest. Okay?"

21

Scott smiled. "Okay."

Del arrived with the stick and handed it to Scott. It was taped near the bottom of the blade and slightly battered.

Coach Roberts blew a blast on his whistle. "Okay, men!" he shouted. "Gather around me a minute!"

The boys skated toward him like a swarm of bees.

"We've practiced a week already, so nearly all of you boys know what to do," said the coach. "We have a new member starting with us tonight. Scott Harrison. He's a good skater, and if we can mold him into a good puck handler I'm sure he'll help our team very much. Skinny, come here beside me. The rest of you line up next to Skinny, with Del Stockton next to last. Scott, you're tail-end Charlie. You follow Del."

The boys hustled into position.

"Okay, follow me," said the coach.

He skated diagonally down the length of the rink toward the corner, circled gracefully behind the goal close to the boards, then skated diagonally across the length of the rink and behind the other goal. He circled that and retraced his path down the rink again and around the goal, the boys following smoothly behind him and copying his every move. Scott realized that the drill taught them to make turns both ways.

He felt an excitement more joyous than he had ever felt skating whichever way he wished on a pond. There was something special about skating with a bunch of hockey players.

The coach suddenly blew a blast on his whistle. Scott, watching Del closely, saw a gap between him and Del quickly widen. He realized then that the blast meant an increase in speed.

He dug his skates hard into the ice. As

he reached the corner and tried to skate smoothly around the curve — one foot crossing over the other in swift, pistonlike motions — the back of his left skate struck the front of his right and knocked him off-balance.

He spun. His knees wobbled. He reached out for something to grab, but there was nothing, and down he went.

Del looked back at him and laughed. "You just lost your membership, speedy!" he cried.

Scott clambered to his feet. "What?"

"Okay, we'll give you another chance," said Del, skating up beside him. "But one more bad goof and you're no longer an Icekateer. Got it?"

3

SCOTT STARED, deeply hurt. Was Del serious? If he was, he's not giving me much of a chance, thought Scott. After all, this is only my first practice. And I have never skated in a drill before.

Skinny eased up beside him when the drill was over. "Don't let Del bother you," he said quietly. "He didn't like the idea of my asking you to be one of us Icekateers. That's why he popped off."

"Maybe I'd better not be," replied Scott. "Not till I can prove to him I'm as good as he is."

Skinny shrugged. "Okay. If that's the way you want it."

"What is the Icekateers, Skinny? A club?"

"No, not really. It's just something special between Del and me. We said that we'd bring in another guy if he was real good, though. That's why I had asked you."

"Hadn't you talked it over first?"

"Well . . . a little." He seemed reluctant to talk about it any further.

"Okay, Skinny," said Scott. "I appreciate your asking me, anyway."

Next came the "skate-the-square" drill. The coach had the boys divide into three teams, placed gloves at eight points on the ice, which, using the face-off spots also as points, formed three squares. Then he had each team skate around a square.

For a while they just skated, the leader

of each team starting off at a slow pace and gradually going faster.

After a while the coach gave the lead man a puck. The man skated around the square twice, then passed the puck to the man behind him.

Here's where I flunk, too, thought Scott.

He watched how each man stickhandled the puck, dribbling it along the ice with quick changes of the stick from one side of the puck to the other — zigzagging it. The closer the puck came to him the more nervous he became.

He watched Del stickhandle the puck like an expert. After skating around the square twice Del backpassed the puck to him.

"All yours, Scott!" cried Del.

The pass was a fast wrist-snap. And Del had shot it a fraction of a second before he had yelled, catching Scott off guard.

27

Scott reached for the puck, but too late. The black pellet zipped past the blade of his stick across the ice toward the boards, and Scott looked at Del.

"That was your second chance, Harrison!" yelled Del. "And you blew it! You know what *that* means!"

Yes, I know! thought Scott. But you wanted me to miss it, you fink! You wanted me to look bad! You hate to see another guy skate as well as you or Skinny!

He sprinted after the puck, intercepted it as it bounced off the boards, then dribbled it up the ice ahead of him. He had done this before while playing shinny, dribbling it back and forth while he skated as fast as he could. He didn't remember ever being nervous before, but he was nervous now. He was tense as a board. Everybody was watching him.

The puck got away from him at the corner.

"Hook your stick around the puck at the sharp turns, Scott!" he heard Coach Roberts advise.

He retrieved the puck, skated straight down to the next corner, then hooked his stick around the puck as he cut sharply at the turn. At the same time he reduced his speed. He made the maneuver without losing the puck and heard the coach say, "That's the way to do it, Scott!"

He completed the circle, went around again, and the coach called the drill to a halt.

"All right. Practice shooting from the blue lines now," he ordered. "Line One on the north goal. Line Two on the south goal. Line Three, rest up till I call you. Scott, stay with Line Two. I want you to work out as a defenseman."

Skinny poked him with his stick and grinned. "You're with us, buddy!" he said.

"Did you see what Del did?" asked Scott.

"I saw him shoot the pass to you," replied Skinny. "Why?"

"He shot before he yelled. He wanted me to miss it on purpose."

Skinny frowned, as if he couldn't believe it.

"I'm not kidding," said Scott. "He did it on purpose. He wanted me to look bad."

"He had no reason to do that," broke in Fat, who had skated up beside him. "I saw that pass. You should've had it."

Scott blushed and suddenly realized that Fat might as well have called him a liar.

"Listen, mister," said Fat, "in this sport you can be a fast skater. But if you're not ready every second you're worthless."

Scott, his face still burning, knew that there was no use saying anything more to

30

either Fat or Skinny. Fat was on Del's side. And Skinny, being an Icekateer, favored Del, too. I might as well keep my mouth shut, thought Scott, otherwise I'll get into hotter water.

He turned and skated along with Skinny to the blue line facing one of the goals, and saw Del Stockton joining them. The other players lining up side by side at the blue line and playing with Line Two were Bernie Fredricks, Joe Zimmer and Vern Mitchell. Paul Carson, a short kid wearing heavy goalie gear, skated to the crease inside the goal. What equipment he had to wear, thought Scott without envy. Leg pads, chest protector, padded jacket, heavy goal gloves. Man! And his stick was really reinforced, too, with white adhesive tape over the heel and partway up the shaft.

The coach gave each line a puck. "Okay.

Start with the man on the left. Dribble to within five feet of the goal and shoot. Follow up on the rebounds."

Del led off for Line Two. He sped toward the goal, dribbling the puck with his head and eyes up, looking at the goal but dribbling the puck as if he were looking at it and the goal at the same time. Wow! thought Scott. No matter what kind of a guy Del was, he could really stickhandle!

Del got to within five feet of the goal, shifted his stick quickly to one side of the puck, then the other, then shot. Paul Carson dove toward the corner where the puck headed like a little black rocket, but missed it.

Bernie Fredricks was next. He dribbled the puck toward the goal, shot, and Paul stopped it with his stick. The puck glanced off toward the boards. Bernie skated after it, caught the rebound, bolted around the

back of the goal and shot again. Again Paul stopped it.

"Okay," said the coach. "Next man."

Paul shot the puck across the ice to Joe Zimmer, who dribbled down, fired at the goal, and missed it. He came around with the rebound and fired again. This time the puck flew over Paul's left shoulder and landed against the net behind him.

"Nice shot, Joe!" said the coach.

Skinny dribbled the puck down the ice like a bullet, zigzagged it as he got near the goal, then shot. The puck skittered past Paul's left skate and against the net.

At last it was Scott's turn. Butterflies fluttered around in his stomach as he dribbled the puck down the ice, got close to the goal and fired it toward the narrow space between Paul's left skate and the side of the net. Paul's foot shot out and kicked the puck toward the boards. Scott raced after it, caught the rebound, and sped around the back of the goal. He saw Paul covering the side of the net like a blanket, and skated by, dribbling the puck with all the experience he had gained while playing shinny on the frozen pond near home.

From the corner of his eye he saw the opening between Paul's legs. Snap! He shot the puck directly through them.

"Nice shot, Scott!" yelled the coach.

Scott returned to the blue line, feeling good.

They continued the shooting practice for twenty minutes. Line Three went in to take Line One's place after ten minutes of play, rested ten minutes, then took Line Two's place. In this way each line had a total of twenty minutes of practice shooting.

They were sweating as they skated off

the ice and into the locker room after the drills. Scott was pooped. Some of the boys bought cold drinks from the automatic dispenser. Scott couldn't. He hadn't brought any change with him.

Skinny came over with two opened bottles. "Here. Take one," he said, grinning.

Scott did. "Thanks!"

Del approached with a soft drink and sat next to Skinny. He ignored Scott completely.

4

COACH ROBERTS gave Scott an approval form to be filled out by his parents and another form to be completed by his doctor after a physical examination. Mom and Dad signed the approval form, which meant that they were letting him play with the Golden Bears hockey team.

At school the next day he asked Buck Weaver if Buck would like to take a vacation from his paper route next week. Buck was a tall kid with hair like straw and a face showered with freckles.

"In this crummy weather I'd like a two-week vacation," said Buck. "Why?"

37

"I need a pair of hockey skates and a stick," replied Scott. "I'd like it for a week. Starting Monday."

"It's yours," replied Buck. "But I've picked up more customers since the last time you went around with me."

"How many have you got now?"

"One hundred and nineteen. I'll keep a cent on each paper, like before."

"It's a deal," said Scott. They shook hands to clinch it.

Right after school Scott took the doctor's form to Dr. Wilkins' office five blocks away. It was snowing and he trotted most of the way. The doctor examined him thoroughly and passed him with flying colors.

"So you're going to play hockey," said Dr. Wilkins, a thin man with a fine-looking crop of black hair slightly sprinkled with gray. His head had been as bald as

38

an egg the last time Scott had seen him. Boy! thought Scott. What a wig can do to a guy!

"It's rough but a lot of fun," remarked Scott, and went out the door. By the time he reached home snow had collected like a thick blanket on his hat and shoulders. He rubbed it off before going into the house, where he removed his rubbers and placed them on a mat.

"Well," said Mom, "Dr. Wilkins find anything wrong with you?"

"Not a thing," replied Scott, pulling off his coat and hat. "Is Dad home yet?"

"It's only four o'clock," said Mom. "He won't be home for another hour and fifteen minutes. Why?"

"Buck Weaver is letting me take his paper route next week. I won't have all the money I'll need to buy a hockey stick and skates till then." He paused. "I was wondering, could you lend me what I need now? I'll pay you back next weekend."

"Of course," said Mom. "I won't lend you money, though. I'll use my credit card. You can pay me when the bill comes."

Scott grinned. "Fine, Mom! Can we get them now? It shouldn't take long."

"Do you know where to go?"

"Yes. Fred's Sporting Goods Store."

"Okay. Put your rubbers and coat back on and I'll get ready."

Footsteps pounded in from the dining room. "Can I go, too?" asked Cathy.

"Me and my shadow," grunted Scott.

"Come on," said Mom.

In less than five minutes they were in the white Volkswagen, rumbling up the street, the windshield wipers snapping back and forth. In another five minutes

40

they were inside Fred's Sporting Goods Store.

Fred showed Scott half a dozen hockey sticks, each with a different size lie. "The lie is the angle of the blade with the shaft, you know," he told Scott. "Try each one. See which fits you the best."

Scott tried each one. They all fitted pretty well. He picked up the third one again, tested it for balance, weight and lie and decided that this was it.

"I also need hockey skates," he said. "Size eight and a half."

Fred lifted a box off the shelf and took out a sharp-looking pair of shoeskates.

Scott tried them on. He stood on a rug with them. They felt great. "I'll take them," he said.

"You've got a good pair there," said Fred. "Should last you through a lot of games. Whose team are you on?"

"The Golden Bears," said Scott.

"Fine. I know your coach. Dick Roberts. Good man. Knows his hockey. Hope you have a good year." He handed the wrapped-up skates and stick to Scott.

"Thanks," said Scott.

He was set now. All he needed was the uniform, and he'd get that from Coach Roberts.

At practice that evening the coach divided the Golden Bears into two teams and had them shinny for fifteen minutes to loosen up their skating muscles. Next was a fifteen-minute period of skating from the blue line toward the goal and then shooting. Then followed a "start and stop" drill during which all the players skated from one end of the rink to the other and back again. Whenever Coach Roberts blew his whistle, the men would come to a quick stop, then start again when the coach gave another blow on the whistle. This drill was supposed to toughen and condition the skating muscles, and develop the sudden stop and start skill.

Scott saw that some of the guys skidded three or four feet before stopping. He didn't. He stopped almost the instant he heard the whistle blow, with both skates turned sharply at an angle, shooting up sprays of ice.

Learning how to bodycheck came next. A lot of the guys knew how already. Scott had seen it done during shinny, but had never really learned the technique.

"Bodychecking is another name for shouldarchecking," explained Coach Roberts. "Keep your body bent forward when you bodycheck or you'll be knocked flat on your back. Keep your legs apart and step into the man you're checking with

your shoulder striking his. Make sure your stick is kept down. If it's up you could hurt him. And whether you hurt him or not the ref could send you to the penalty box for high-sticking."

He dropped the puck on the ice. "Del, go after it," he said.

Del did. The coach leaned forward. Just as Del passed the puck with his stick, the coach rammed into Del's left shoulder with his right, knocking Del back.

"That's how it's done," he said. "Except that you'll get hit much harder. Or, if you're doing the bodychecking, you will *hit* much harder. Okay, Scott, go after the puck. Del, bodycheck him."

Scott skated toward the puck as he had seen Del do. He kept shifting his eyes from the puck to Del and back to the puck, wondering just how hard Del would hit him. Just as he reached the puck and struck it, Del bolted into him.

45

The surprise blow from the right shoulder instead of the left, and the hard contact, knocked Scott back. He lost his balance and went down. The guys burst out laughing.

Scott rose to his feet, red-faced. Del grinned.

"Cut the laugh," said the coach. "Scott, he surprised you by hitting you with his right shoulder. That's why you went down. You were also looking down and up from the puck to Del, waiting for him to bodycheck you. Now, listen closely. The time to bodycheck a man is when he least expects it. Just when he passes the puck. Del," he said, tossing the puck some five feet in front of him, "go after it. Bodycheck him, Scott."

Del went after the puck, his stick held out in front of him. Scott shot forward like an uncoiled spring. Just as Del's stick blade touched the puck Scott hit Del's shoulder with his left shoulder, and stopped Del cold.

"Good work, Scott!" cried the coach.

Scott saw Del's surprised look and turned away, a faint smile playing on his face.

"Boys," said the coach, "once you're in uniform I want you to work on bodychecking all you can. It's one of the techniques that helps make a good defensive team. Okay. Let's head for the locker room. Got something for you."

What he had for them were in boxes piled up beside a row of lockers. He tossed a box to each man, whose reaction was a loud, happy yell before tearing open the box and yanking out its contents — a gold uniform with black trim and white numbers.

Scott held his up proudly, then turned

it around and looked at the number on the back of the jersey: 12.

"Pretty neat," said a voice beside him. "Think you can earn it?"

Before Scott could answer, Del Stockton walked away.

5

SCOTT REMEMBERED every one of Buck Weaver's customers except the new ones Buck had picked up, and Buck had given him addresses for these. The temperature was down around thirty-five on Monday, but the sun was shining.

He made the deliveries on foot and in two trips. The first trip was to the customers at the right of his house, the second at the left. The total delivery time was one hour and fifty-two minutes. He kept track by his wristwatch.

That night was devoted to hard drills: skating frontwards and backwards, shooting at the goal with long and short shots, quick starts and stops, bodychecking and, finally, scrimmaging.

He avoided Del as much as he could. He felt guilty doing so, since it was partly because of Del that he was on the Golden Bears' team.

Being close to Fat McCay bothered him, too. But Fat greeted him with a soft "Hi," and Scott returned the greeting, hoping that no rift would develop between them. He didn't want to risk losing Skinny's friendship over a silly argument with Fat.

Coach Roberts played Scott at right defense, Joe Zimmer at left defense, Bernie Fredricks at right forward, Skinny McCay at left forward, Del Stockton at center on Line Two. Paul Carson was the goalie.

They started the scrimmage against Line One with Coach Roberts acting as referee. Line One's center, Art Fisher, was two inches taller than Del. But when the coach dropped the puck in the face-off Del showed that what he lacked in height he had in speed.

He grabbed the puck with a quick flash of his stick, dribbled it past the red middle line, and snapped it to his left wingman, Skinny McCay. Skinny grabbed it and dribbled it across Line One's blue line. Bill Thomas, Line One's chunky right defenseman, bodychecked Skinny and sent him spinning. He then passed to his center, Art Fisher, who dribbled the puck a bit then passed it across the red line to a teammate skating hard down center ice.

Scott saw the play coming the moment he saw Art looking for a receiver. The teammate was Buggsy Smith, Line One's fast left forward. Buggsy reached for the puck as it sizzled across the ice toward him, but he never got it.

Scott had hooked it with his stick. He brought the puck around in front of him, started to dribble it forward, and crash! Someone struck him like a ton of steel. A shower of stars splashed up in front of him like a Fourth of July celebration and he fell. He sat there, waiting for the stars to vanish. In a few seconds they did, and he saw Bill Thomas taking off with the puck.

"Hurry up, Scott!" shouted Coach Roberts. "Cover your position!"

He clambered to his feet and sprinted toward the net. Left defenseman Joe Zimmer was skating hard after Bill, and so were the two wingmen, Del Stockton and Bernie Fredricks.

Bill shuffled the tiny black disk back and forth as he got near the net, then gave it a quick wrist-snap. Goalie Paul Carson, jerking his large stick back and forth in front of the net to match Bill's quick movement, wasn't fast enough to stop it. The puck sailed past him and into the net for a goal.

"H'ray!" shouted the Line One players.

Scott started to circle back to his position at right defense and saw Skinny Mc-Cay swing around in front of him.

"You okay?"

"Yeah."

"All right!" yelled Coach Roberts. "Line Two, out! Come in, Line Three!"

Scott glanced over at Del as the six men of Line Two, including the goalie, skated off the ice. Del's head was down. He seemed deep in thought.

I know what he's thinking, thought Scott. *He's wishing that he and Skinny had never asked me to play with the Golden Bears.*

The scrimmage lasted another twenty

minutes. The boys assembled in the locker room, took off their skates and put on their shoes.

"We'll scrimmage every night this week except Friday," announced the coach. "Most of you are pretty green yet. You need a lot of polishing up. See you tomorrow night."

He saw them the next night, the next and the next. On Thursday night he had the team devote the evening to scrimmaging between the lines. Line Two, on the ice with Line Three, got the puck from face-off as Del socked the disk across to his left wingman, Skinny McCay.

"Watch that hanger!" yelled a Line Three man.

Scott looked and saw Bernie Fredricks standing near the red line, a few feet behind and to the left of a Line Two defenseman.

The warning came in time. Skinny shot the puck to Bernie, but a second defenseman had spun about, intercepted the pass, and was dribbling it back down the ice.

Scott sprinted toward him. When he was within six feet in front of the puck carrier, the man brought his stick far back and swung it in a vicious arc at the puck.

Without thinking, Scott covered his face and closed his eyes. He waited for the sound of the stick smacking the puck. Instead, he heard the quick scraping of skates. He dropped his arm and opened his eyes.

Where the defenseman had stood was now an empty space!

Scott glanced toward the goal, just in time to see the man sprinting toward it. Snap! Like a bullet the puck shot past Paul Carson's legs and into the net.

A yell rang out from the members of

56

Line Three. They jumped and hollered as if this were a real league game.

Suddenly their voices died. Scott saw the guys look at each other, say something, then look at him.

"You freaked out, Scott!" Del yelled at him. "You really freaked out!"

Scott stared at him. "What?"

"What?" echoed Del. "You're puck shy, that's what!"

Scott stood as if frozen.

The league games hadn't even started yet and he was already knee-deep in trouble with Del Stockton. Now something new had sprung to make his playing hockey that much tougher.

He was afraid of the puck.

6

THE FACE-OFF.

Fat McCay, center for Line Three, beat Del to the puck and passed it to David Wink, his left wingman. David dribbled the puck across the blue line and then the red line, then passed it to Fat who was skating hard down center ice.

Fat hooked the puck with his stick, shoved it to his left and began to dribble it toward the corner.

"Get it, Scott!"

Scott recognized Del's voice.

"Sure! Get it, Scott!" echoed Fat.

Scott saw the smile on his round, red-cheeked face. Fat was small and chunky, the exact opposite of Skinny. But his skill on the ice was deceptive. He was faster than he looked.

Scott bolted after him, his stick stretched forward to poke check the puck. Just then Fat yelled, "Look out!" and pulled back his stick to belt the puck.

Scott covered his face and closed his eyes. He couldn't help it. He waited for that sound — the sound that would tell him that Fat had smacked the puck.

Instead, laughter exploded close to him, followed by the sound of skates *phut-phutting* by. He saw Fat dribbling the puck toward the goal, no one in front of him except the goal tender, Paul Carson.

Fat zigzagged the puck as he headed for the crease, the square in front of the net, then passed the disk to a man coming from the opposite direction.

Snap! Thud! Just like that the man snapped the puck between Paul's left skate and the corner of the goal and scored.

Again there was a thunderous cry from the men of Line Three. And again Scott saw them looking at him. Looking and smiling as they had done before.

And then he saw Del skate up beside him, his eyes like white rings.

"You did it again, speedy!" he blurted.

Scott blushed.

"When Fat motioned to swing at the puck you covered your face and closed your eyes!" said Del. "Fat saw you do that before when somebody else faked a swing at the puck! So he did it and look what happened! He went by you and you didn't even know it!"

60

Coach Roberts skated up to them. "What's the trouble?"

"No trouble," said Del, and skated away. Scott headed for his position at right defense.

"Scott," called the coach.

Scott swung around in a quick arc and pulled up in front of Coach Roberts.

"Was he talking about you covering your face when Fat faked a swing at the puck?"

Scott nodded, so ashamed he wished he had never seen a hockey puck.

"Well, don't get sick over it," said the coach. "It happens to some players. You'll just have to condition yourself to stop doing it. Okay. Go to your position."

Scott wasn't able to put himself entirely into the scrimmage after that. He couldn't erase the expression of Del's face from his mind, nor those terrible words: *Puck shy.*

He was glad to get home that night.

The next day he hated to go to school, but he had to. He couldn't tell Mom or Dad why he wanted to stay home. They wouldn't understand.

Puck shy? they'd say. *You must be kidding. You mean that you'd stay home because your friends would laugh at you for being a little afraid of the puck? That's ridiculous!*

Grown-ups just don't understand those things.

Time went by quickest during classes. It was the first day that he ever enjoyed classes more than study periods.

That night he rolled and tossed in bed, thinking about the game tomorrow and about Del Stockton. The Golden Bears were playing the Grayhawks, their first game of the season. All he could think of was skating pell-mell toward a puck, then stopping dead cold and covering his face as an opponent pulled back his stick to take a swipe at the little black pellet. And of Del yelling at him. Humiliating him.

What hurt so was that the whole team — all the Golden Bears — knew about his fear, too. How could he play hockey — good hockey — knowing of his weakness?

Somehow he slept. After breakfast he put on his hockey uniform and helmet, got his stick, skates and gloves, and rode with his mother, father and Cathy to Cass Rink.

He kept mum every bit of the way. Once Mom said, "Nervous, Scott? Can't blame you. It's natural. I'm not playing, but I'm probably as nervous as you are."

He didn't say anything.

There was nothing said in the locker room about him. You would think the guys had forgotten all about his puck shyness.

The game started at exactly ten o'clock.

Art Fisher, Line One's center for the Golden Bears, got the puck in the face-off from Jack Young, the Grayhawks' center, and passed it to right wingman Jim Lamont. Jim dribbled it down the ice close to the boards and lost it when a man in a silver uniform with red trim, the Grayhawks' colors, rammed into him in a neat bodycheck. The puck was loose for a few seconds, rolling toward center ice.

A Grayhawk reached it, lifted his stick, swung. The puck rose off the ice and headed like a rocket directly for the Golden Bears' goal. Goalie Cary Small lifted his left gloved hand and caught it.

"Great save, Cary!" yelled the Bears' fans.

Face-off. This time Jack Young won possession of the puck, shot it to a wingman, and sped toward the goal. Golden Bears chased the Grayhawks' wingman

around the back of the net, where he was met by a Golden Bear coming from the opposite direction.

He snapped the puck against the boards. It bounced off, shot toward Jack Young. Cary Small never saw the puck as Jack slapped it past him into the net for a goal.

At the end of four minutes a bell sounded, and Line Two of both teams took over. Scott inhaled deeply as he stepped onto the rink and to his position.

The face-off.

The dropped puck triggered both teams into action. Scott waited tensely, watching the little black disk being struck, poke checked, slapped, and snapped.

Suddenly it shot down the length of the ice. Scott and Joe Zimmer bolted after it. Scott intercepted it behind the net. At the same time the ref's whistle pierced the air and icing was called.

The face-off was between Del and a Grayhawk at the other end of the rink. Sticks clattered. Then Del struck the puck, sent it smack against the boards to his left. It bounced back, directly toward Skinny McCay. At the same time Scott crashed against the boards as a Grayhawk slammed into him. His helmeted head banged against the wall, jarring him.

A whistle stopped the play as the ref waved the offending Grayhawk to "jail" for boarding.

"You want to watch that headhunter, Scott!" yelled Skinny.

Scott smiled. Headhunter was right.

Face-off. Skinny got the puck, dribbled it into Grayhawk territory. He passed to Del. Del caught it, dribbled it toward the goal, shot.

A save!

Del got the puck in the face-off and passed to Skinny. Skinny bolted for the goal, zigzagging the puck with quick movements of his stick, then shot.

The puck sizzled across the ice, banged against the goalie's outstretched skate, and skittered toward the boards.

Scott saw his man charge for the puck and skated after it, too. He flashed by the man and started to reach for the puck. Another Grayhawk popped up from behind the net, stick drawn back to whack the puck.

Scott, only a few feet away from the disk, wanted to go on. He wanted that puck. But a bolt of fear rattled him. The puck had turned into a missile, ready to fly at him.

He covered his face with an arm, and shut his eyes. It was only for a second or

two, but time enough for the Grayhawk
to slap the puck past him.

"Scott!" Del's voice thundered. "Want
a mask?"

7

COACH ROBERTS pulled him off the ice and put in Vern Mitchell, the sub.

"Afraid of the puck hitting you, aren't you, Scott?"

Scott's heart was pounding. "I think so."

"The fact is, the puck rises off the ice very seldom," said the coach. "The way it's hit prevents it from rising. Even when a guy pulls back his stick to give the puck a hard whack the chance for it to fly off the ice is slim. Better work on that, Scott. You saw what happened the other night during scrimmage. The boys caught on to your being puck shy. They scared you out of a play and scored. The Grayhawks will do the same thing the minute they catch on."

"They probably did on that play," said Scott softly.

"I wouldn't be surprised."

At the ten-minute time the buzzer sounded again. The two lines went off the ice and Lines Three of both teams went on.

Fat McCay was center for Line Three. The Grayhawks' center was a head taller than Fat, and about twenty pounds lighter. He looked as if he could skate circles around Fat.

But it was Fat who got the puck. Fat who passed it to a wingman. Fat who caught a pass down center ice, dribbled the puck past two defensemen, and then

71

slapped it past the goalie for the first score of the game.

A thunderous shout, mixed with a hard banging of hockey sticks against the boards, sprang from the Golden Bears.

Fat was watched carefully after that. With a minute to go before the three minutes were up Fat tripped a Grayhawk with his stick. Even though he argued with the ref that he had not done it on purpose, he was sent to the penalty box for one minute.

The Grayhawks took advantage of the five-man team and tied the score, 1 to 1.

Line One couldn't break the tie.

Line Two couldn't, either. Scott was so worried that he might do what he had done before that the coach took him out after a minute and a half and put in Vern Mitchell.

"You're worried about it, now, Scott,"

72

said the coach. "You'll have to settle down."

When the next minute and a half were up, Line Three of both teams got on the ice. This time it was Fat McCay again who scored, putting the Golden Bears ahead, 2 to 1.

The boys sucked on lemons in the locker room during intermission. Coach Roberts perked them up with a short speech, telling them that they "were doing a good job. After all, we're ahead by one goal, and all they got against us is one. So what can I say? Fat, you're doing fine. Just keep it up."

The game resumed. It looked as if the first four minutes would go by scoreless until a surprise slap shot within the last thirty seconds made by the Grayhawks' center, Jack Young, tied the score, 2 to 2.

"Okay, Scott," said the coach as Line

Two went in, "keep your mind on the game. Don't worry about the puck."

The face-off. Burt Stone, centering against Del, got the puck and passed it to a wingman. The wingman dribbled it over the blue line and into Golden Bears territory, flakes of ice spraying from his skates as he sprinted toward the goal.

Joe Zimmer went after him. The Grayhawk skated away from him, and headed directly toward Scott. Scott started to poke-check the puck when the Grayhawk pulled back his stick and started to take a vicious cut at it.

Again the puck turned into a little black monster. And again Scott raised his arm and shut his eyes.

The whistle shrilled, loud and piercing. Scott opened his eyes, dropped his arm, and saw the ref skating toward him, looking and pointing directly at him!

74

Scott stared.

"High-sticking!" boomed the ref. "The penalty box, fella!"

It was then that Scott realized that this time he had raised his stick-hand to protect his face. He had gone from bad to worse.

8

SCOTT HARRISON had to sit in the penalty box for a minute. He was more ashamed than angry. Of all the hockey players he knew only he was shy of the puck. The thing was, he *tried* to keep from lifting his arm. He *tried* to keep from shutting his eyes. But just at the moment when the opponent was going to swing, he'd lose control of himself and seek protection.

"Okay, Scott," said the timekeeper. "Minute's up."

Scott bolted out of the penalty box and onto the ice, determined not to let the puck get the best of him again.

"Let's get on the ball, huh?" said Del, glaring at him.

Del's words, and tone of voice, rattled him. Never had anyone bothered him as much as Del did.

Even Fat's "Come on, Scott! Let's go!" didn't affect him half as much. And it was only because it was Del who, with Skinny, had asked him to join the Golden Bears, thinking that he would be a great help to the team. Instead, he was a burden.

But he wouldn't quit. No one was going to call him a quitter. Even if I never become the good hockey player Del had expected me to be, I'll never quit, he promised himself.

He stayed behind the blue line at the right side of the rink, waiting for the puck to come his way. For thirty seconds Bernie, Skinny, Del and Joe were fighting for control of the puck against the five Gray-hawks. Suddenly Skinny got it and drib-bled it hard behind the net. Grayhawks scampered after him from both sides. Just as one of them was about to poke check the puck Skinny banked it against the boards. Del intercepted it, sped toward the net, and slammed it. The Grayhawk goalie fell in front of it for a beautiful save.

Scott saw Vern Mitchell come onto the rink and skate hard toward him. *Here I go*, he thought.

He skated off the ice.

"You're worried about doing the same thing," said the coach as Scott sat down. "You'll just have to work on it, buddy. It's the only way."

The buzzer announced the end of the three minutes and the lines went off, re-placed by Lines Three. Fat almost shot one in after forty seconds of play, but the Grayhawk goalie caught it with his gloved hand.

The Grayhawk center, Jack Young, got control of the puck at face-off and dribbled down center ice. Just as Del swooped upon him to poke-check the puck, the Grayhawk hit it and sent it flying like a rocket through space. It grazed past goalie Steve Hatrack's ear for a goal.

Grayhawk sticks boomed against the boards. They were ahead, 3 to 2.

The Golden Bears fought hard to tie it up, but couldn't. At the end of the game the Grayhawks won, 3 to 2.

In the locker room Scott hurried to get his skates off and his shoes on. He didn't want anyone reminding him of his trouble.

But someone did. Del Stockton.

"I wouldn't believe it if I didn't see it," he said. "You . . . a great skater . . . puck shy!"

"I can't help it," said Scott, his heart pounding.

He got up and started out.

"I just can't believe it," said Del, staring after him.

Scott glared at him. "I heard you!" he cried angrily. "Now leave me alone, will you?" He left the building.

Dad and Mom talked about his problem at home. "Why can't he wear a mask?" suggested Mom.

"Oh, Mom," Scott glowered. "None of the other guys wear masks. Only the goalie. I'll get over it."

Mom looked reflectively at Dad, as if she were wondering whether Scott would or not.

"It's a peculiar reaction," explained Dad. "And I agree with Scott. If he's determined to get over it, he will."

Thanks, Dad, he thought.

He rested after dinner, then telephoned Skinny and asked him if he'd like to play shinny at the ice pond.

"Sure, said Skinny. "I'll bring some guys with me. Okay?"

"Okay," said Scott.

He walked to the frozen pond above the falls, taking along his hockey stick and a puck. Cathy went along. They had walked half a block when a shout came from behind them. Pete Sewell came running up, carrying his skates over his shoulder.

"Hi!" he greeted. "I saw your game this morning, Scott. You played pretty well."

"Right," said Scott. "Just pretty well."

Skinny, Fat, Steve and three other guys

showed up at the pond, and they chose up sides for a game of shinny. Skinny and Fat did the choosing. *Watch,* thought Scott, *I'll be the last one chosen.*

They used a hockey stick to determine who would choose first. Fat tossed it to Skinny. Skinny caught it near the middle. Fat wrapped a hand around it above Skinny's. Then each put his hand above the other's until the top of the hockey stick was reached. The person whose hand covered the stick's end chose first. Skinny won.

Without looking to see who was around him, Skinny said, "Scott Harrison."

Scott couldn't believe it.

Fat chose Steve Hatrack. Finally all the players were chosen. Fat had first choice for the goal and took the one on the falls side. Goals were made simply from small rocks set about five feet apart, one placed some forty feet from the edge of the falls, the other placed where the river narrowed like the shape of a bottleneck. This provided a playing area about sixty feet long.

There was no boy nearby to act as referee, so Cathy volunteered. The boys looked at her suspiciously for a while, and Scott smiled.

"Don't worry about her," he said. "All she has to do is drop the puck in a face-off."

The teams got into position. Skinny and Fat were centers for their teams. Cathy dropped the puck. The centers' sticks clashed with it, and the game was on.

Fat's stick jabbed the puck and sent it skittering across the ice toward the side. Steve bolted after it, hooked it with his stick and dribbled it toward his goal — the goal that was next to the falls. Scott skated after him, came up from behind, and Steve passed to another team member. Scott then sped after him, determined to steal that puck.

Just as he started to reach for it a second opponent came in from his right side and gave him a bodycheck that knocked him off balance. He went down, skidded, got up quickly, and again went after the puck.

A teammate skated up from his defensive position and forced the opponent to turn sharply to his right. As he did so, he saw Scott coming at him. Quickly he raised his stick and brought it down to strike the puck.

Scott shut his eyes, started to lift his arm. And then remembered. *No!* he thought. *I won't get hit by the puck! I won't!*

In that fraction of a second the man struck the puck. It flashed past Scott like a bullet. Scott turned and sprinted after it.

On a rink the play would be icing, for the puck was heading to the left of the goal. The goalie was chasing after it, but he was like a turtle after a rabbit.

Scott skated as fast, or faster, than he had ever skated before. He knew that the falls were just over that curved edge, but the puck was slowing up. He felt sure he could get to it before it reached the edge.

He soon realized that he couldn't, and a wave of horror swept over him. He saw the puck disappear over the edge of the frozen falls. He lowered his body and tried to turn around in a circle to clear the dangerous edge.

He didn't make it. The edge of his skates got too much of a bite in the ice, and he was thrown off balance.

A loud, ear-piercing yell split the air as he left the ice and went hurling through space.

9

THE YELL stopped when he saw the swirling white foam rush up at him. He struck the roaring, gushing foam head first. Even as he went under and felt the cold water swallow him he kept his eyes open.

He went down . . . down . . .

Then he began to stroke and kick hard to get to the surface. His clothes and skates were heavy on him. They, and the falls striking the water above him, kept him from rising to the surface. He thought that he would never see daylight again.

His lungs ached for air. He wanted so

much to take a breath, but he knew that doing so would only fill his lungs with water and he might drown.

He looked up and saw water gushing down through the frothy surface, and thousands of air bubbles rising and popping above him. He would never make it to the surface here. The plunging falls would just force him back down.

He swam past the falling water and the bubbles. And, just when he felt his lungs were ready to burst, he broke out of the water, sucked in the cold, fresh air. Although he was wet and freezing, he was so happy he wanted to shout. And he did.

Then he swam to shore, his body feeling as though it weighed a ton. He crawled on his knees to the jagged ice that lined the shore, then got up and walked onto the hard-crusted snow.

Skinny and Fat were the first to reach

him. Behind them came Cathy, her face white as the snow.

"Come on," said Skinny, grabbing his arm, "we've got to get you home."

Fat grabbed his other arm. "You do that for kicks?" he asked.

Scott thought his face would crack as he forced a smile. "Just thought I'd go sw-swimming for a change," he said.

Cathy's watery eyes looked at him. "You — you okay, Scott?"

"I'm f-fine," he stammered.

"Skinny, you're the fastest here," said Fat. "Get his shoes."

While Skinny ran after Scott's shoes, Scott sat on a log and Fat and Cathy took off his skates. Skinny arrived with the dry shoes and the boys put them on.

Scott shivered as he got to his feet and started to run, Cathy beside him. "Better

90

call a doctor the minute you get home," advised Skinny.

Scott arrived home and thought Mom would faint when she saw him in clothes that were caking over with ice.

"Scott!" she screamed. "What happened to you? Get into the bathroom! Take off those clothes and get into the tub as quick as you can!"

"He fell over the falls," explained Cathy.

"Over the *what?*" cried Mom.

"The falls," said Cathy.

Scott got out of his ice-caked clothes and into the tub. He sat shivering in it while he turned on the faucets and waited for the tub to fill. He was still in it, and beginning to feel warm and comfortable, when there was a knock on the door.

"Scott, Dr. Wilkins is here," said his mother's voice.

He climbed out of the tub and, with the towel wrapped around him, he opened the door. Dr. Wilkins smiled at him.

"Well, hello, Scott. You get thawed out?"

Scott grinned. "I think so," he said.

"Let me give you a bodycheck, anyway," said the doctor. "This one won't hurt. Put on your shorts and lie on your bed."

Ten minutes later Dr. Wilkins was taking a small glass container out of his black case and putting it on the nightstand beside Scott's bed.

"Give him two now, then one every four hours until they're all gone," he said to Mrs. Harrison. "And keep him in for the next couple of days."

Scott stared at him. "But Dr. Wilkins, I feel okay!"

The doctor smiled. "This stethoscope tells me different. Don't worry. By Tuesday you'll be good as new."

Tuesday was a long time coming.

10

SCOTT PRACTICED with the Golden Bears at Cass Rink on Tuesday, and realized that recuperating for two days had taken some of the strength out of him.

He felt stronger on Wednesday, with one thing on his mind above everything else: *I must stop being afraid of the puck. That's the only way that I can get Del and the rest of the Golden Bears feeling that I'm really one of them.*

The team had intrasquad scrimmage, the lines taking turns playing against each other. The moment that Line Two went in against Line One Scott felt the excitement bubble inside him.

He watched the puck drop from Coach Dick Roberts' hand in the face-off, watched Del Stockton knock it across center ice toward the opposite goal only to be intercepted by Buggsy Smith.

Buggsy dribbled it back across the center line and then socked it hard as Bernie Fredricks scooted at him from the side, his stick stretched out for the puck. Bernie hit Buggsy and both crashed against the boards.

The puck skittered down the ice toward the goal, Scott Harrison and Joe Zimmer bolting after it together. Scott reached it first and belted it back up the ice. An instant later he saw Del Stockton cross in front of him, glaring hotly.

"How about passing it once in a while?" yelled Del.

Scott flushed. In his anxiety to strike the puck up the other end of the rink he had forgotten to look for a receiver.

"The puck, Scott!" someone yelled.

Scott ducked and saw the puck skitter-tering toward him. He hooked it with his stick and dribbled it across the blue and then the center lines. An opponent rushed at him from his right. He put on more speed and stickhandled the puck expertly down the left side of the ice while at the same time he looked for a teammate to pass to.

Del was covered. So were Skinny and Bernie. One man stood in front of the goal, protecting it with the goalie.

For a moment he thought, Should I head for the goal and try a shot? Why not?

He bolted forward. Left defenseman Al Podeski charged at him and tried to slap the puck. Scott stickhandled it away. He faked a shot to Del, who stared as if to say, *Don't pass now, you nut!*

Then Scott skated past the crease in front of the defenseman guarding it. Without slowing up he turned to his right and at the same time snapped the puck past the defenseman's legs, and the goalie's, into the net.

"Well! You did it, man!" yelled Del.

Scott grinned shyly as he skated back down the ice to his position, realizing he had done something probably few of his teammates had noticed. He had scored while skating backwards, a feat he had learned only within the last two weeks.

Coach Roberts blew his whistle and called in Line Three to play against Line Two. "Fine skating, Scott," he said. "Rest awhile; I want Vern Mitchell to get in some practice, too."

The following two nights put him in good shape for Saturday's game against the Beetles. Their name, *Beetles,* and a drawing of a beetle were in bright red on the front of their black satin jerseys.

After a minute and eleven seconds of play Art Fisher knocked in a goal. Thirty seconds later Buggsy rapped one in between the goalie's legs to put the Golden Bears in front, 2 to 0.

Fourteen seconds before the three-minute time was up the red light went on behind the Golden Bears' net for a Beetle score: 2 to 1.

The buzzer sounded. Lines One left the ice and Lines Two came on. The face-off. The scramble for the puck. Scott saw it skitter on its edge toward his side of the rink and sprinted after it. He didn't see the Beetle going after it until both of them were within five or six feet of the puck.

He stretched out his stick. At the same

time the Beetle pulled back his and swung at the puck. For a very brief instant Scott sensed what could happen and lifted his arm. *You're doing it again!*

He dropped his arm. By then the Beetle's stick had swung and struck the disk, sending it like a black bullet down the ice.

"Chicken!" yelled Del as he zoomed by Scott.

Just then a Beetle brushed by him, striking his stick. The impact knocked his stick against another kid's leg. Del's!

Del swerved and came at him, his eyes blazing. He pulled up in front of Scott, his face only inches away, so close Scott felt his warm breath.

"I'm sorry," said Scott. "It was an accident."

"Accident! Yeah!"

"Come on, you guys!" yelled Skinny. "Let's play hockey!"

They broke apart, and Scott saw that

goalie Paul Carson had stopped the puck with his stick and was tossing it to the referee. The ref skated toward the circle to the left and in front of the goal, and waved Skinny McCay and a Beetle to come forward.

The face-off. The battle for the puck. Skinny batted it against the boards and it ricocheted back onto the rink toward the center line. Del scooted after it, dribbled it across his blue line, and passed to Bernie. Bernie nabbed the pass and shot.

A save!

Face-off again. The puck skittered toward center ice. A Beetle belted it. Swish! Down the length of the rink went the puck!

Scott got it behind the net. The whistle shrilled and the ref took the puck to the opposite end of the rink for the face-off.

A Beetle pass! A teammate intercepted

100

it, dribbled down the ice, then shot. The puck blazed past Scott's legs. He stuck out his stick, but too late. The puck whisked between Paul Carson's outstretched foot and the goal post for the Beetles' second score.

Scott looked at the face that suddenly came into his view.

Say it! he thought. Tell me I should've stopped that shot!

But Del didn't say a word.

11

FACE-OFF.

Del Stockton's lightning moves got the puck away from Stinky Marsh, the Beetles' center. Del dribbled it across the Beetles' blue line and was met head-on by two Beetles.

He shot the puck to Skinny McCay skating up from his left side a second before the Beetles crashed into him. Down went all three of them.

Skinny sprinted for the goal, ice spraying from his skates as he stickhandled the puck. Scott, hovering behind the center line, saw a Beetle swooping toward

Skinny, leaving the area behind him wide open. Realizing that this was a good chance to get the puck and try for a goal, Scott bolted forward.

"Skinny!" he shouted.

Skinny snapped the puck. It skittered across the ice toward Scott, who was already skating toward the goal. He stopped the puck with the blade of his stick, took a couple of long, hard strokes, and snap! The Beetle goaltender almost did a split as he kicked his left foot out to stop the streaking puck.

He missed. Goal!

"Nice play, Scott!" cried Skinny, smiling.

"Thanks for the assist," Scott grinned.

Golden Bears 3, Beetles 2.

The face-off. This time Stinky Marsh's fast moves got the puck away from Del. He passed to a teammate, who started to dribble the puck up the center of the ice.

Scott charged after him. The Beetle smacked the puck, sending it whizzing past Scott. Scott sprinted after it, stretching out as far as he could reach with the blade of his stick.

Crash! Down went a player as he tripped over the stick. A Golden Bear!

Oh, no! groaned Scott. It was Del again!

Del went skidding across the ice against the boards. He sat there, glaring at Scott, who skated to him.

"Sorry, Del," Scott apologized, holding out a hand. "I didn't see you."

"Get outa here," muttered Del as he scrambled to his feet.

A second later there was a loud roar, followed by the banging of sticks against the boards, from the Beetles' side. They had scored a goal to tie up the score, 3 to 3.

"They can thank *you* for that," grunted Del.

Scott's heart ached. Del was right. But this time Del should've seen my stick, he told himself. He just couldn't brake in time so he puts the entire blame on me.

Seconds after the face-off the buzzer rang. Lines Two skated off and Lines Three skated on.

"You two are getting pretty reckless out there," observed Coach Roberts bluntly. "What's the matter with you guys?"

"Nothing," said Del.

"I can smell that lie a mile off," replied the coach.

Del's face colored. "He tripped me."

"Tripped you? Why would he want to trip you?"

"I've been yelling at him."

105

"Oh. Why?"

Del shrugged. "He's been making mistakes."

"So? Haven't I been trying to correct them? Or do you think you can do a better job by yelling at him?"

Del looked straight ahead, his ears beet-red. "No, I don't," he admitted. "I'm sorry."

"And I'm surprised," said the coach. "Didn't you and Skinny bring Scott into the club?"

Del nodded.

"I don't know," sighed the coach. "Maybe you're not pleased with Scott's performance. But this is his first season. You've got to give him a chance. Okay. Let's drop the matter right now. One of the easiest ways of losing a hockey match is to have at least two members of the same team cross sticks with each other.

106

Let's end that of this minute. Okay?" He paused. "Del?"

"Yes, sir."

"Scott?"

"Yes, sir."

"Fine."

They watched the remaining minutes of the game between Lines Three in silence. Lines One took over, and the Beetles knocked in another goal, putting them in front, 4 to 3.

"Let's get 'em back," said Skinny as the buzzer sounded and Lines Two replaced Lines One on the ice.

Face-off. The puck dropped. Sticks clashed. Skates blazed across the ice. Here and there black satin uniforms mixed with the gold. Suddenly, a crash at the side boards. The *Phreeeeep!* of the whistle. Scott saw a Beetle down on the ice, Del Stockton on top of him.

A fight? No. Boarding. One minute in the penalty box. Del rose and skated off, his head drooped.

It was five men against six now. The face-off. The fight for the puck. It skittered toward the boards. Scott, Bernie, Skinny and two Beetles sprinted after it.

Scott, faster than the rest, reached it first. He hooked it with the blade of his stick, spun around, and dribbled across the center line, then the blue. He looked up, saw the Beetle goaltender crouched in front of the goal, legs apart, stick held ready. On each side of him was space.

Scott fired. The puck sailed like a rocket toward the right of the goalie. The goalie's hand snapped at it like the tongue of a frog snapping at a fly. He missed.

Goal!

Thunder resounded as Golden Bear sticks banged against the boards. "That-away to go, Scott!"

Golden Bears 4, Beetles 4.

Again the face-off. Again the struggle for the puck. Then the minute was up. Del came back on the ice. The Bears skated brilliantly. They bodychecked, passed, shot, and shot again. The buzzer sounded. It was time for Lines Three.

Three minutes later the first period was over. The score was still 4 to 4.

"Nice shooting, Scott," said Skinny as they headed for the locker room.

Scott smiled, and looked for Del. Their eyes met for a moment, then Del looked away.

They quenched their thirst with soft drinks and sucked on slices of oranges while Coach Roberts looked proudly at them.

"You guys are playing good hockey," he said. "You're skating fine. A little shy about taking shots, but that's okay. Pass a little more. And pass in *front* of your

110

man, not at him. Watch yourselves about boarding as Del did. Boarding, charging, or illegal bodychecking are violations."

The second period started.

Lines One got on and off without scoring. The Beetles' Line Two threatened in the first thirty seconds when Stinky Marsh belted the puck against goalie Paul Carson's skate from just beyond the crease. The puck ricocheted toward the boards, only to be picked up by Stinky again.

Skating brilliantly he dribbled behind the goal. Scott, suspecting what Stinky was going to do, skated in front of the crease to help Paul defend the goal. Stinky swooped around the corner of the net, brought his stick back, and let it fly at the puck.

Scott saw it leave the ice like a rocket and head for him. He lifted his arm, closed his eyes and ducked.

Crack!

12

THE PUCK STRUCK his helmet and glanced over the net against the boards.

Scott stood frozen, his heart pounding. The thought of what had happened hit him, and he sucked in his breath and held it. Around him black and gold uniforms were flashing every which way. A Beetle bumped him. He spun, fell.

A gold uniform appeared before him. He looked up into Skinny McCay's face. "Scott! You okay?"

He nodded, and tried to rise to his feet. His knees were rubbery and he fell again.

Phreeeeep! The whistle brought the blur of gold and black uniforms to a stop. The ref skated forward, helped him to his feet, and guided him off the rink. Coach Roberts met him at the gate.

"Scott, you hurt?"

"No."

He was dizzy. He wanted to sit down. The coach helped him to the bench. "Take it easy," he said. "You'll be all right."

He sat down. In a while his head cleared. He saw that Vern Mitchell was in his place, and felt ashamed. He was breathing easier now, but his heart was still pounding and sweat was dribbling down his cheeks into the corners of his mouth.

The coach unsnapped his helmet, took it off, wiped the sweat off with a handker-chief.

"Just relax and watch the rest of the

113

game from the bench," he advised. "You played a good game. You showed a lot of spunk."

"I showed that I'm still scared of the puck," murmured Scott.

"That's all right. You'll get over it. But it takes more than one game, or two games, or even three. It's not easy."

"I'll never get over it," said Scott.

"That's crazy talk, kid. You think you're the only one who's ever had that problem? Some pros have it, too. Yes, pros. I know. I've seen them."

Stinky Marsh scored a half a minute before the three-minute time was up. Fat McCay tied it up when Lines Three went in, but it was Stinky again who later broke the tie. And that was the way the game ended. Beetles 6, Golden Bears 5.

Coach Roberts met Dad and Mom at the exit door.

"Hi, Dick," said Dad. "How's Scott? Think we should keep him off the rink for a while?"

Scott's heart jumped to his throat. He looked from his father to Coach Roberts.

"No. I don't think we ought to get him away from the game entirely. I'll just watch him. Leave him to me."

The coach met Scott's eyes and he winked.

"There's practice Monday at six-thirty," he said. "Can you be there?"

Scott smiled. "Yes."

13

SCOTT and Cathy went to the pond Sunday after church and skated till noon. Scott saw that Cathy was keeping a safe distance away from the falls and smiled to himself. He knew she was doing it so that he wouldn't go near them himself.

Don't worry, he thought. *Once over those icy falls is enough!*

That afternoon they rode with Dad and Mom in the country. The roads were clear and the snow-covered trees stood erect and still in the white fields. They passed snowmobiles that glided swiftly over the fields, leaving twin trails behind them.

Passing by a mountainside they watched skiers riding on a ski lift to the top of the mountain and skiing down the long, slanting slope. Halfway down, one of the skiers fell, lost a ski, and skidded nearly to the bottom of the hill before he got back on his feet.

It was nearly dark when they returned home. Mom and Cathy put supper on the table and Mom cooked hot chocolate and they ate and talked about the things they had seen.

Scott went to Cass Rink on Monday evening. The Golden Bears practiced skating backwards for fifteen minutes, then worked on bodychecking and hip-checking (bumping the side of the puck-carrier with your hip to knock him off stride), passing and shooting. The last half hour was devoted entirely to scrimmage.

117

The following evenings their practice routine remained the same. By game time Saturday Scott thought he had really licked his problem.

The Golden Bears played the Bullets. When Lines Two took over the ice from Lines One in the first period the score was 1 to 0 in the Bullets' favor.

The Bullets wore gray, red-trimmed uniforms with white letters and numbers. A picture of a bullet with wings on it was on the front of their jerseys. Slim Jason was their center.

The face-off. The dropped puck. The two hockey sticks batting at it. Then Slim struck it solidly, sending it across the Golden Bears' blue line.

Joe Zimmer intercepted it and dribbled it back up the ice. A Bullet rushed at him and Joe passed to Scott. Scott stickhandled the puck across the red line into Bullet territory, saw a Bullet sprinting toward him, and passed to Del. Del shot, missing the goal by a foot.

A Bullet retrieved the puck behind the goal and dribbled up the ice.

"Get back!" Del yelled at Scott.

Scott spun, saw that all five Bears, including himself, had left their side of the rink wide open. He started to skate backwards, his eyes on the puck-carrier. But the Bullet had picked up speed and was sprinting down the side. Scott turned and sped after him. He reached out to hook the puck. The blade of his stick caught the Bullet by the ankle, and down he went.

Phreeeeep! went the whistle.

"Nice going!" Del grunted as he skated by.

The ref motioned Scott toward the penalty box, then skated there himself. "Tripping," he said to the timekeeper.

The Bears tried hard to keep the puck down in Bullet territory, but, with twenty seconds remaining of Scott's penalty, Slim Jason blasted a shot past goalie Paul Carson into the net.

The Bullets had the puck in their possession when the timekeeper turned to Scott. "Okay. Time's up."

Scott rushed out onto the ice, eager to make up for that lost minute.

He seemed to have surprised the puck-carrier, for the man glanced around at him wide-eyed as Scott sneaked up from behind him, bodychecked him aside, and stole the puck.

He dribbled the disk across the center line and the blue line with Bullets on both sides of him. He saw Skinny come into his view at his left and passed the puck to him. The pass was good. Skinny caught it with the blade of his stick, dribbled toward the Bullets' goal, and wrist-snapped it.

Goal!

Golden Bears' sticks clattered against the boards. "Nice shot, Skinny!" yelled the fans.

Del skated up beside Scott and smiled. "Nice play."

"Thanks," said Scott, who thought, *That's the first nice thing he's said to me in ages.*

The buzzer sounded and the lines skated off, giving the ice over to Lines Three. The Bullets' line proved stronger than the Bears' and scored twice before Fat McCay got hot and banged in two to tie it up again, 3 to 3.

Buggsy assisted with a score and shot one in himself to put the Bears back in the lead, 5 to 3.

Lines Two went back on the ice.

Hardly six seconds ticked off after the drop of the puck when Slim Jason smashed a line drive directly for the goal. The puck shot like a small black meteor at Scott, who was in its way. For the first time in a long time the little black puck turned into a little black monster.

It was shooting directly for his face.

14

SCOTT DUCKED.

At the same time he knew that if the puck sailed by him it might shoot past Paul Carson for a goal.

He raised his hand. *Smack!*

The puck struck the pocket of his glove, clung there for just a fraction of a second, then dropped.

"Nice stop, Scott!" yelled Del.

Golden Bears' sticks clattered against the sideboards, and just for a second Scott Harrison smiled. He felt good.

A Bullet sped toward him, hockey stick held out to grab the puck. Like a shot Scott dropped his stick and flicked the puck to Del, whom he saw skating up at his left.

Del caught the pass and dribbled it across the center and then the blue line into Bullet territory. Two Bullet defensemen went after him. Del passed to Skinny and Skinny shot. The puck blazed through the air like a rocket, but the Bullets' goalie stuck out his gloved hand and stopped it.

This time Bullet hockey sticks rattled the sideboards, and cheers rang out for their goalie. "Nice save, Ed!"

Skinny and a Bullet defenseman stood ready for the face-off in the circle at the front left of the Bullets' goal. The puck dropped and Skinny got control of it almost instantly.

He sprinted toward the goal. A guard struck him with a bodycheck, knocked him to the ice, and the puck skittered toward the goal crease. Another guard hooked it with the blade of his stick and whisked it away up the center of the ice.

Scott back-skated hurriedly to cover his zone. Del went after the puck-carrier, who passed to a teammate skating near the sideboards several feet in front of Scott. Scott stopped back-skating and shot forward. Just as he started to reach for the puck the Bullet pulled back his stick and swung.

Scott clamped his eyes shut and raised a hand.

No! No! Quickly he opened his eyes and dropped his hand, in time to see the puck whizz past his legs.

The buzzer sounded, ending the three minutes. Lines Two went off, Lines Three went on.

Scott expected Del to remind him of what he'd done, but Del didn't. Nor did Coach Roberts.

Neither team of Lines Three scored and the buzzer sounded, ending the first period.

While Scott sucked on a slice of orange Skinny, sitting beside him, said softly, "Scott, Del ever tell you who really wanted you to play with us?"

Scott frowned. "Wasn't it you?"

"No. It was Del. He'd seen you skate and thought you were the best he'd ever seen."

"You're kidding."

"Ask him," said Skinny.

Scott stared at Skinny a long minute. "I guess I've really disappointed him," he said. "No wonder he acted like he did."

Someone tapped him on the shoulder. He turned and saw that it was Del. Del smiled as he tossed a sucked-out slice of orange into a rubbish can and wiped his mouth. "Not anymore," he said, smiling.

"You sure?"

Del's smile spread. "Look, I think I've learned to keep my mouth shut when I'm supposed to. Oh, by the way, Skinny and I decided we want you with us again."

"As an Icekateer?"

"Of course!"

"Come on, boys!" interrupted Coach Roberts. "On the ice. Hustle!"

Lines One created a lot of action on the rink, but that was all. Lines Two continued the action, with one difference: Slim Jason scored to put the Bullets one point behind the Golden Bears, 5 to 4.

Fat McCay fouled twice for Line Three, keeping him out most of the three minutes and giving the Bullets an opportunity to score twice, going ahead of the Bears, 6 to 5.

"Our last time around," Scott said to Del as Lines One shot the puck all over

128

the rink for three minutes without getting a good shot at the net. The buzzer sounded and Lines Two took over.

"And this is our last chance," said Del. "How do you feel, Scott?"

"Fine."

"Good. Let's knock in a few."

The face-off. The dropped puck. The fight for it. The clatter of sticks. And then Slim Jason had the puck, dribbling it down center ice, ice chips flying from his skates as he sped. He was stickhandling the puck with one hand, zigzagging the disk with speed and the greatest of ease.

Skinny tried to steal the puck away from Slim's right side, Del tried to poke check it from his left. Both Bears were good hockey players, but Slim was better. He was fast, graceful, confident.

And then Scott, covering his zone close to the front and right side of the rink, saw it coming. Slim's stick was rising. He was going to shoot.

Just as his stick hit the puck Scott sprinted in front of the goal, directly in line of its path.

Fear gripped him as he saw it coming at him. But he didn't panic. He didn't shut his eyes. He didn't duck.

Instead, he lifted his hand, stopped the puck, dropped it, then sent it spinning across the ice toward Del. Hockey sticks thundered against the sideboards on the Golden Bears' side.

"Beautiful stop, Scott!"

Scott skated up the ice after the puck. There was a scramble for it, then several shots for the goal. None went in. Moments later the buzzer sounded, and the lines left the ice, replaced by Lines Three.

There was little said on the bench as Lines Three battled for three minutes without scoring. The game ended in the Bullets' favor, 6 to 5.

"No disgrace to lose," said Coach Roberts in the locker room. "You all played an excellent game. Forget this one. There's a new game next week."

"Think you're over being puck shy?" Skinny asked Scott.

"I got a little scared that last time," admitted Scott.

Del looked at him, smiled. "It takes a lot of guts to admit that," he said.

Scott shrugged and put on his shoes. He swung his shoeskates over his shoulder, stood up, and started for the door.

A shout from Del exploded behind him. "Hey, wait for us! We're the Three Icekateers! Remember?"

He smiled as Del and Skinny came up beside him, and together they walked out of the building.

How many of these Matt Christopher sports classics have you read?

- ❑ Baseball Flyhawk
- ❑ Baseball Pals
- ❑ The Basket Counts
- ❑ Catch That Pass!
- ❑ Catcher with a Glass Arm
- ❑ Challenge at Second Base
- ❑ The Counterfeit Tackle
- ❑ The Diamond Champs
- ❑ Dirt Bike Racer
- ❑ Dirt Bike Runaway
- ❑ Face-Off
- ❑ Football Fugitive
- ❑ The Fox Steals Home
- ❑ The Great Quarterback Switch
- ❑ Hard Drive to Short
- ❑ The Hockey Machine
- ❑ Ice Magic
- ❑ Johnny Long Legs
- ❑ The Kid Who Only Hit Homers
- ❑ Little Lefty
- ❑ Long Shot for Paul
- ❑ Long Stretch at First Base
- ❑ Look Who's Playing First Base
- ❑ Miracle at the Plate
- ❑ No Arm in Left Field
- ❑ Pressure Play
- ❑ Red-Hot Hightops
- ❑ Return of the Home Run Kid
- ❑ Run, Billy, Run
- ❑ Shortstop from Tokyo
- ❑ Skateboard Tough
- ❑ Soccer Halfback
- ❑ The Submarine Pitch
- ❑ Supercharged Infield
- ❑ Tackle Without a Team
- ❑ Tight End
- ❑ Too Hot to Handle
- ❑ Touchdown for Tommy
- ❑ Tough to Tackle
- ❑ Undercover Tailback
- ❑ Wingman on Ice
- ❑ The Year Mom Won the Pennant

All available in paperback from Little, Brown and Company

Join the Matt Christopher Fan Club!

To become an official member of the Matt Christopher Fan Club, send a business-size (9 1/2 x 4") self-addressed stamped envelope and $1.00 to:

Matt Christopher Fan Club
c/o Little, Brown and Company
34 Beacon Street
Boston, MA 02108

Books by Matt Christopher

Ice Magic

ICE MAGIC

Matt Christopher

Illustrated by Byron Goto

Little, Brown and Company
BOSTON · NEW YORK · TORONTO · LONDON

Library of Congress Cataloging in Publication Data

Christopher, Matthew F.

  Ice magic.

  Summary: The twins' toy hockey game seems to be magic as it plays
games identical to the real ones before they even happen.

  [1. Hockey—Stories]   I. Goto, Byron   illus.
II. Title.

PZ7.C458Ic   [Fic]   73-4885

ISBN 0-316-13958-0

ISBN 0-316-13991-2 (pbk.)

HC: 10 9 8

 PB: 15

VB

Published simultaneously in Canada
by Little, Brown & Company (Canada) Limited

Printed in the United States of America

To Dale and Joanne

Ice Magic

1

THE MORNING of Saturday, December 1, was unlike any other morning ever in Pie Pennelli's life.

It started with a laser beam shooting at his right eye. The blinding light startled him. Then he realized that it wasn't a laser beam at all but the sun shining through a hole in the drapery of his bedroom window.

He had been dreaming.

He moved over in the bed, hating to leave its soft, velvet warmth. But he knew he would have to soon. The Fly League

3

hockey game started at eight o'clock and he had to be at the rink a half hour before, at the latest.

As if thinking about it was a signal, there came a sudden knocking on his door and his mother's vibrant voice. "Pie! Get up!"

"Okay," he grunted softly.

He got up, washed, put on his black and white hockey uniform and had breakfast.

"Better hustle," his mother said. "You've got only eight minutes to get to the rink." He smiled at his blond, trim mother, and as he stood up, noticed with disappointment that she was still a head taller than he was.

"I'll make it," he said, and looked at his father, a lean, broad-shouldered man with a moustache. "You going, Dad?"

"Can't this morning," Mr. Pennelli said. "I've got to work on the car. Who are you playing?"

"The Bears," Pie answered. "They're real good."

"So?" His father's dark brows arched. "Be better."

Pie shrugged, remembering that Dad used to say the same thing to Pat. Pie's older brother, now at State College, was one of the best defensemen in the business. It was Pat's ice skates Pie was using. They were about two sizes too large, but Dad said he couldn't afford buying a new pair. "Your feet will grow into 'em," he had told Pie.

"By then I'll be in high school," Pie had answered.

In the meantime he had to be satisfied with them, but even laced up tightly they

6

felt like canal boats and slowed down his playing.

He flung the skates over his shoulders and went to the door. "See you later," he said, and stepped out into the bone-chilling air.

He walked up Oak Street, crossed Madison and turned left, soon reaching the high wire fence that separated the street from the gorge that gave the village of Deep Gorge its name. Just past the gorge the fence turned up at a right angle to form a protective wall between it and a path going up the steep, tree-dotted hill. A squirrel chattered as it clung, head down, onto the side of a tree that hung over the breathless chasm, and Pie smiled.

"Morning, squirrel," he nodded.

He arrived at Davis Rink and Terry — Terry "the terrible" Mason — saw him and looked up at the clock. A crooked smile came over the tall, dark-haired boy's face.

"Eight-thirty on the button," he said. "One more second and you would've been late."

Like Pie's brother, Pat, Terry also had a brother going to State College. Both Pat Pennelli and Bob Mason were competing for a position on State's hockey team.

"A second is as good as an hour," Pie snorted.

"The way you played last week I really believe it," Terry said. "What do you do Friday nights? Watch the late-late show?"

"And the late-late-late show, too," Pie replied, exasperated. He hadn't sat down yet to put on his skates and Terry was already picking on him.

Last week Terry had done the same thing, picked on him throughout the entire game. *How can I play a good game*

8

of hockey with him riding me all the time?
Pie thought.

He didn't know why Terry was so crusty toward him. He wished he knew, but he didn't.

Ten minutes before game time both teams got on the ice and skated round the rink to limber up their leg muscles. The Bears wore brown uniforms with white trim and white helmets with a brown stripe across the center. Only a handful of fans sat in the stands that seated a capacity crowd of three thousand.

Up on the electric scoreboard the time clock read 12:00. The first of the four large glass buttons beneath the hour lights was lit. Each button designated a period. The game was comprised of three periods. The fourth button was lit in case of a tie score, and that was used only when the high school played.

The buzzer crashed through the sound of gliding, slithering skates. The two referees blew their whistles, and like flies both teams scrambled off the ice, leaving only their first lines.

The Penguins protected the north goal. In front of the net was goalie Ed Courtney; at right forward, Pie; at left forward, Bud Rooney; at center, Terry "the terrible" Mason; at right defense, Chuck Billings; and at left defense, Frog Alexander. Watching from behind the boards stood Coach Joe Hayes, wearing a baseball cap and yellow-rimmed glasses. Beside him sat the rest of the Penguin roster.

Phreeet! went the whistle, and the ref dropped the puck.

Terry and Ed Kadola, the Bears' belligerent center, slapped at it and it skewered across the ice to Bud. Pie sprinted down the ice, looking over his shoulder for a pass. *Slap!* Down it came as Bud shot the puck to him.

Pie hooked it with his stick, saw Terry backskate toward the Bears' net, and was about to fire the puck to him when a Bears defenseman bodychecked him. Another Bear stole the puck and slapped it hard to the other end of the ice. And Pie heard Terry yell, "You slowpoke! We could've scored!"

Almost on the heels of Terry's chaffing remark came a yell from the stands. "Come on, Pie! Show 'em!"

He didn't dare waste time looking up to see who the rooter was, but the voice sounded familiar.

Then another voice yelled his name, and this one he recognized. It was Coach Hayes. "Get down to that blue line, Pie! Hurry!"

He dug the point of his right skate into

the ice and bolted toward the line. Across
the red center line the Penguins' two defensemen were struggling to wrest the
puck away from the Bears' forwards. Suddenly the puck shot to the side, rammed
against the boards, and bounced on its
edge toward the corner.

Terry and a Bear hightailed after it.
Both reached it at the same time, collided
and fell. Terry, on his feet first, hooked
the blade of his stick around the puck,
dribbled it behind the Penguins' net, then
shot it up the ice.

"Pie!" he yelled.

Pie caught the pass, turned and headed
up the ice toward the Bears' net. His feet
seemed to be swimming in his shoes, and
he wished again that he was wearing a
pair that would fit snugly. He *knew* he
could skate a hundred per cent better
with tighter fitting shoes.

He saw the Bears' defensemen charging toward him, and he pulled back his stick, aiming to sock the puck at the space to the right of the Bears' goaltender. *Swish!* He missed the puck completely. Then *crash!* Down he went as the two defensemen plowed into him.

Stars danced in front of his eyes as he landed on the ice, both Bears on top of him. The whistle shrilled. The Bears rolled off him, and he climbed slowly to his feet, groggy and tired.

He skated off the ice with the rest of Line 1 and felt a sharp blow against his right elbow. He turned. It was Terry, his face shining with sweat.

"Why don't you take up tumbling?" he said. "You seem to do that pretty well."

"I'll think about it," said Pie as he stomped through the open gate. He found a space on the bench and sat down.

He wasn't going to tell Terry or anyone else about his oversize skates. They'd laugh him out of the rink.

For two minutes the second lines of both teams fought but had no success in knocking the puck into the net, and for another two minutes the third lines tried unsuccessfully, too. It wasn't till the first lines went back in that a Bear broke the scoreless tie.

Then the Penguins knotted it up when Terry "the terrible" Mason, after driving down the ice from the red center line, socked the puck up into the corner of the net unassisted.

The rink resounded with a roar as jubilant Penguins drummed their sticks against the boards.

Five seconds after face-off, Pie caught a pass from Bud Rooney, bolted toward the Bears' net and saw his chance to score. The Bears' goalie had slipped to one knee at the right side of the crease and was taking his sweet old time getting to his feet.

Smack! The puck streaked like a black pellet through space. Up shot the goalie in a futile effort to catch it with his gloved hand.

Goal!

"Nice shot, Pie!" the familiar voice shouted again in the stands.

This time he recognized it, and a grin curved his lips. He looked up at the sea of faces and saw two that looked exactly alike — the Byrd twins, Jody and Joliette.

Jody waved. "See you during intermission!" he yelled.

"Can't!" Pie yelled back.

"Your fans, Pennelli?" a voice sneered near his elbow.

He turned sharply and read Terry's mocking grin.

"My friends, if you'd like to know," answered Pie and turned his attention to the game, which continued without another score to the end of the first period. Penguins 2, Bears 1.

Pie clambered off the bench and skated off the ice, plagued by his oversize shoe-skates more than he was by Terry's cutting sarcasm.

Tired and half worn out, he stepped into the locker room, sat down, and took off his helmet. The cool air felt refreshing. He was ready to settle for a few minutes of much needed rest, when in burst a couple of kids, both in blue snowsuits and both looking as alike as twins could possibly look.

"Pie!" Jody Byrd cried breathlessly.

"It's coming out exactly like we thought it would!"

"Exactly!" Joliette repeated.

Pie stared from one bright-eyed, red-cheeked face to the other. "What is?" he asked bewilderedly.

"The game!" Joliette cried. "It's coming out exactly the same!"

Pie frowned. "The same as what?"

Just then Terry Mason's voice cut in like a sharp-toothed saw. "Hey, you kids, beat it. Even the great Pennelli's fans aren't allowed in here."

The twins scowled at him and headed for the door. "See you after the game, Pie."

Pie nodded, still frowning. *The same as what?* he thought. *Just what were those twins talking about, anyway?*

17

2

FACE-OFF, and the second period was underway.

Terry Mason and Ed Kadola smacked at the puck. It skittered toward left forward Bud Rooney who socked it across the ice to Pie. Pie stopped it, dribbled it across the blue line, saw a Bear defenseman charging at him and passed to his right defenseman, Chuck Billings.

Bang! Chuck clouted the puck toward the Bears' net.

The Bears' goalie shifted his left leg and stopped it with his pad. He then picked it up and tossed it behind the net, where another Bear retrieved it and started to dribble it up the ice.

Crash! Pie bodychecked him at the boards as he tried to pokecheck the puck. *Phreet!* sounded a whistle, and Pie saw a ref pointing at him.

"Boarding!" the ref yelled. Pie shook his head and skated off the ice toward the penalty box.

"You went at him like a bomb," said Terry, skating up beside Pie. "You can't take more than two steps when you're checking a guy. Don't you know that?"

Pie glared at him. "I wasn't thinking about steps," he grunted. "I was thinking about getting that puck."

"Well, you'd better think about steps, too," Terry snapped.

Pie found it difficult to control his temper, and was almost pleased for the one-minute penalty. While he sat serving his sentence, the Penguins tried desperately to keep possession of the puck. They knew that if the Bears got it they could try a power play, and the Penguins, with five men on the ice instead of six, could do very little about it.

And that's what happened. A Bear stole the puck from Frog Alexander and all five of their men — the goalie remained at his position — kept control of the puck. They passed it back and forth among them, evading Bud, Terry, Chuck and Frog with quick, accurate passes.

Then *snap!* A goal!

Ed Courtney picked the puck up dejectedly and tossed it to the ref, while the huge room thundered with the resounding noise of hockey sticks drumming against the boards.

Penguins 2, Bears 2.

The ref waved Pie back onto the ice. It was a ruling that a man serving a penalty was permitted to get back into the game if the opponent scored a goal.

Ten seconds later the two-minute session was up and Line 1 skated off the ice. Line 2 accomplished nothing, but the Bears' Line 3 broke the tie when their center bombed one in from the blue line.

The Penguins' Line 1 took the ice and threatened to score over a dozen times, but the Bear goalie's fantastic saves stopped them every time.

Going into the third period Pie had his best chance of the game to chalk up a point. He had intercepted a pass from a Bear and was sprinting down the ice toward the Bears' goal with not an opponent near him.

"Score, Pie! Score!" a shout rose from the stands.

He had reached the right side of the net and was less than five feet from it. He saw the goalie crouched there like a wall, legs spread apart, the big stick on the ice in front of him. But at his right side was a clear, wide-open space, and that was where Pie hoped to direct the shot.

He had to make his move now. He had to shift quickly to the left, sweep in front of the goalie and shoot.

He shifted his skates, pointing them to the left in front of the crease in the direction he wanted to go. Then something happened. His feet had turned, and so had his skates. But not far enough. The combination of oversize shoes and momentum made it impossible for Pie to turn in time, and he went crashing into the goalie.

The whistle shrilled. Disgruntled, he disentangled himself from the goalie and

crawled out of the crease. He wasn't hurt, but he couldn't tell whether the goalie was. The face mask hid any sign that might be on the guy's face.

But it didn't hide the look in the guy's eyes, the sparks of anger shooting from them.

"I'm sorry," Pie said apologetically.

He saw the ref pointing at him and then at the penalty box. "Charging!" the man in the striped shirt announced.

And once again Pie had to serve a one-minute sentence.

"You had it made, man!" yelled Terry. "And you blew it!"

You would have blown it too if you were in my shoes, Pie wanted to tell him.

Again the Bears used a power play to take advantage of the six men against five on the ice, and again they scored.

Pie came back on the ice filled with the determination to get that score back, and he managed to drive a shot that missed the net by inches. He could skate reasonably well forward, backward, and to the left and right, and he wouldn't commit a foul or lose his balance as long as he didn't attempt any sudden turns. But Pie knew that he had to make fast moves to score and that those sudden turns would always be his pitfall.

The two minutes were up and Line 2 came in. Center Rusty Carr scored with an assist by left forward Bob Taylor at 9:17 on the clock, then scored again unassisted. Penguins 4, Bears 4.

Line 3 failed to score but played excellent defense, keeping the Bears' third line from flashing on a single red light.

Pie, back on the ice for the second two-minute session of the period, blew another chance of scoring when Terry passed him the puck from the corner behind the Bears' net. Pie stopped the pass with the blade of his stick and started to dribble closer to the net, only to be bodychecked by a Bear and have the puck stolen from him.

"Pie!" Terry yelled. "Why didn't you shoot?"

Pie's face turned red. He realized now that he should have shot the instant he had received Terry's pass. *Man!* he thought. *I'm glad Dad isn't here to see this!*

Fifteen seconds later the Bears' Ed Kadola scored with an assist by his right forward. Then a Penguin blasted one in from the blue line to tie up the score, 5 to 5.

While the second line was on the ice, Terry said to Pie, "We're going on the ice one more time. Hope you don't do anything to get yourself in the sin bin."

"You think I *want* to get in there?" Pie snorted.

"Well — you *play* as if you do," Terry answered, bluntly.

Neither Line 2 nor Line 3 could break the tie, and Line 1 returned to the ice for its last chance. Pie remembered Terry's curt warning and tried his best not to commit a foul. He realized, though, that being careful didn't help either. Once, instead of charging toward a Bear to intercept a puck, Pie slowed down and let the man receive the pellet without trouble. Maybe, he thought — just maybe — the man might miss the puck.

He didn't. He hooked it neatly with his

stick, passed it to a teammate, and a score followed.

"Pie!" Terry shouted at him. "Why didn't you stop him?"

Ignoring him, Pie skated to his position, sullen and dead tired. *Man, I just can't do a thing right,* he thought dismally.

It was Line 2 that tied up the score again, and then Line 3 that broke it, winning the game for the Penguins 7 to 6.

They shouted joyously over their victory, and their fans cheered, too. Pie hoped that the win would make Terry forget how he had performed today. But he was sure it wouldn't. Even though Terry ignored him completely as they headed for the locker room, Pie knew that Terry never forgot someone else's mistakes — only his own.

Pie put on his shoes, slung the skates

over his shoulders, and walked out to the snow-packed street. The bright sun dazzled like a diamond through the bare trees. The frigid air nipped at his cheeks like sharp teeth.

"Hi, Pie!"

Jody and Joliette Byrd sprang from behind a bush to surprise him and laughed when he jumped.

"You crazy kids," he said. He remembered the strange comment they had made to him in the locker room immediately after the first period of the hockey game, and asked, "What were you guys saying about a game?"

"Our toy hockey game!" Jody replied, getting on Pie's left side while Joliette got on Pie's right. They both were at least a foot shorter than he, and it embarrassed him every time they greeted him this way.

Some guys had kidded him about having these little kids as friends.

But they had one thing in common with Pie which made him care less what anybody thought. It was their mutual interest in magic. Since the twins had found an old book on magic in their attic and had let Pie read it, all three of them had become so interested in the subject that they had purchased new books. Jody even said that he would become a magician when he grew up.

"And I'll be his assistant," Joliette had promised with that teeth-flashing smile of hers.

"What about the toy hockey game?" Pie asked curiously.

"Well, Jolie and I played a game last night," Jody explained. "We named the teams the Bears and the Penguins, and I had the Penguins. I also named each of the players after each of the guys on the Penguins' team."

"So?"

Jody looked at him seriously. "We played and my team won 7 to 6."

"What a coincidence," said Pie. "That was our score!"

"Right," Jody said. "But that isn't all. The guys who had scored on my team were the same ones who had scored on yours — it's like magic!"

3

PIE STARED, his mouth a small round "o." He had read a lot about magic. There was the entertaining kind in which a magician pulled doves out of his coat pockets or made a person disappear in a puff of smoke.

There were also magical spells which believers thought could make rain when crops were poor.

And there was black magic, too — in which believers thought they could hurt a victim by sticking darts into a doll which they pretended was the victim.

But this thing with the toy hockey game

was different. This was a kind of magic Pie had never read about before.

"Are you sure that all that stuff in our game really happened in yours?" he asked the twins. "Really sure?"

"Of course, we're sure," Jody replied emphatically. "Remember that last period when that Bear scored against you?"

Pie nodded. "When I let him take the puck because I was afraid I might plow into him and be called for a penalty."

"Right. Well, I had you do the same thing in our game," said Jody. "Except that I was hoping that Jolie would miss it, and I could take it from her."

Pie stared. "That's exactly what *I* had been thinking!" he cried.

The twins' expression matched his. "You had?" they asked in the same breath.

"Yes!" said Pie, and felt his nerves tingling.

They reached the junction opposite the gorge and turned right on Oak, none of them saying a word during the last one hundred feet. They were immersed in the toy hockey game which seemed to be controlled by some kind of magical power. It wasn't like anything the three had ever read about before in their lives.

"I'd like to see that game," Pie said at last. "Mind?"

"Of course not. Why don't you come over right after you change?"

"I will," said Pie. "And look — don't spill a single word about this to anybody. Not even your parents. Okay?"

Joliette laughed, "Are you kidding? They wouldn't believe it anyway! Mom thinks all that magic business is just a trick!"

"And Dad doesn't know *what* to believe!" Jody added, laughing.

Pie chuckled. "I guess our parents are very much alike," he said. "My mom and dad used to like magic when they were kids. Now they think it's kid stuff and pay no attention to it."

Pie arrived home and promised the twins he'd be over in an hour or so. They lived next door, which made their visiting each other to talk about their mutual interest — books on magic — very convenient.

"Hi, Mom," he said as he stepped into the kitchen. "What've you got to eat?"

Those were the first words he always greeted her with when he returned from a grueling hockey game. Nothing ever made him hungrier than a tough game of hockey.

"Hash browns, eggs and bacon," she said, and asked, "Who won?"

"We did. 7 to 6."

He hurried to his room, took off his uniform, showered, then dressed and returned to the kitchen. His meal was ready for him.

His mother watched him gulp it down. "Where's the fire?" she asked.

He smiled. "At Jody and Jolie's," he answered kiddingly.

After he finished he went over to the Byrds' house, and the twins invited him into the small recreation room in the basement where the toy hockey game was set up on a table. It was about eighteen inches wide and thirty-six inches long. On it stood four-inch high plywood figures that were maneuvered by rods protruding from the narrow ends. Clearly the figures were hockey players, each holding a hockey stick. Goals, made of cloth, were at both ends of the "rink."

Pie stared at it. "It looks handmade," he observed.

"It is," Jody replied. "There's a name carved on the side of it. Look."

He lifted the game and saw a crudely carved name: SKXROT. After it was a number, 1896.

"S-K-X-R-O-T," Pie read. "That's a peculiar name. 1896. That must be the date this thing was made."

"Really? Was hockey played that many years ago?" Joliette asked, incredulously.

"Oh, sure," Pie said. "It started — " He paused and stared at the date again. "That's sure funny," he said half to himself.

"What is?" Jody asked.

"I've got a copy of the *Official Hockey Guide,* and I'm sure I read that the first official ice hockey game was played in 1896!"

"Oh, man!" Jody whistled. "Weird!"

"I — I feel shivers crawling up my back," Joliette stammered, clasping her hands so tightly together the knuckles turned white.

Pie took hold of the knobs of each rod protruding from the ends of the game and began pushing them back and forth, thereby manipulating the players in the slots on the rink. A twist of the knobs one way or the other turned the players, making them hit the miniature puck.

"It's just like games you can buy in stores," Pie remarked. "Except this one is real old."

"You should've seen it when we found it," Jody said. "It was covered with dust."

A wooden, inch-high wall surrounded

the rink. There was a box in one corner where the score was kept. The only thing the rink lacked was a red light like the one that flashed on in a real rink when a goal was scored.

"Look at this," Jody said, handing Pie a rolled-up piece of paper that had yellowed with age. "It was wrapped around one of the rods with a rubber band."

Pie unrolled it and saw a neatly printed, four-line paragraph.

To whom it may concern: This hockey game is endowed with magical powers. However,
Beware what happens on a real rink first
Repeats here not, for fate
Promises that, as true as bubbles burst,
The magic will dissipate.

Pie read the message again, then murmured, "Hmm. This is the strangest thing I ever saw."

"Us, too," said Joliette. "And it is magic. We proved it."

"I wonder if anybody else had ever played it," Pie said.

Jody shrugged. "I don't know. It was stuck in a far corner of the attic. I wouldn't be surprised if we were the first."

"Could be," said Pie. "Well, let's play a game."

They sat at opposite sides of the game and began to play. Pie had difficulty manipulating his men as rapidly as Jody did, and after ten minutes of play Jody won, 5 to 1.

During all that time Pie looked for something strange about the toy hockey game, something that would prove to him that it definitely had magical powers. But he saw nothing, and in spite of the message that the twins had found with the game, he began to doubt its genuineness.

If he weren't so sure that the twins were sincere believers in magic, he'd think they were pulling his leg.

He was sure they were sincere, though. The expression on their faces when they had first told him about the real game was plenty of proof.

He was sure, too, that they wouldn't pull a mean trick on him about such matters. Magic to them was a real, wonderful thing, and they loved it. You don't pull practical jokes about something you love.

"May I come over before our next hockey game?" Pie asked. "I'd like to see if it'll work like the first time."

"Sure, you may," replied Jody.

"Maybe it won't work if you play it," Joliette said, her blue eyes looking at him avidly.

"Then I'll watch you guys play," Pie said.

42

4

ON FRIDAY Pie went next door to the Byrds' house and knocked on the door. No one answered and he knocked again. Still no one answered.

"Hi, Pie," said a voice behind him. "Aren't your little friends home?"

Pie turned and saw that it was Terry "the terrible" Mason. A calico cat was at his feet, sitting on its haunches and looking at Pie with large, yellow eyes.

"I guess they aren't," Pie said, and started off the porch.

"I heard that you and the twins are really uptight about magic," Terry said, an amused glint in his eyes. "That right?"

"That's right," agreed Pie.

Terry chuckled. "Why don't you use magic when you're on the rink? You could be the greatest."

Pie forced a smile. "Maybe I don't want to be the greatest," he said. "But I suppose *you* would."

Terry shrugged. "Why not? What's wrong with being the greatest?"

Pie considered. "Nothing, if you don't let it go to your head."

The cat at Terry's feet suddenly rose on all four paws and looked across the street. Its tail swished back and forth, and Pie looked up. What had caught the cat's attention was another cat.

Two cars were coming down the street, one behind the other, and for a moment Pie held his breath. *Does Terry see what*

44

could happen, or should I warn him? he thought.

Too late! The cat leaped off the curb and started to run across the street!

"Tipper!" Terry yelled.

There was a loud screech of tires on asphalt as the first car tried to come to a sudden stop. Then, *Bang!* The second car rammed into it.

By now Terry was running after the cat, Pie behind him. They saw it limping off the street on the other side, favoring its right hind leg. It reached the curb, lay on its side, and began licking the wounded limb.

Terry knelt beside it. "You dumb cat!" he scolded. "You want to get killed?"

Pie watched Terry take hold of the leg and stroke it gently and tenderly, and he suddenly saw a part of Terry that sur-

45

prised him. Sarcastic and humiliating though Terry was at times, he was kind and merciful to a dumb animal.

He looked up as the two drivers came running from their cars. "How's the cat?" the first man asked anxiously.

"His leg was hit," said Terry.

"Want me to take him to a vet?"

"No, thanks. I'll take care of him. He'll be all right."

"You sure?"

Terry nodded. "I'm sure."

"Okay. But watch him, will you? He might not be so lucky the next time."

They left, stopped to look at the rear of the first car, carried on a brief discussion, then got into their vehicles and drove away, waving as they went by.

"Guess neither car got damaged," Pie said.

"Glad about that," Terry replied, then turned his attention back to his cat. "You dumb cat, if I have to get a leash for you I will," he said gruffly.

He picked it up, held it close in his arms, and walked away. Pie watched. You'd think that Terry wasn't even aware that he was there.

5

AS USUAL, Pie arrived at the rink the next morning with one minute to spare. And, as usual, Terry "the terrible" Mason had a remark for him.

"Hi, early bird. Why'd you get here so soon?"

Pie ignored the sarcasm, believing that it was the best way to handle Terry. "How's your dumb cat?" he asked.

Terry shrugged. "He'll be okay. No broken bones or anything."

"Good."

Pie put on his skates and got on the rink

with the rest of the team. He wondered if the twins had played with their toy hockey game last night. He looked up at the stands but didn't see them.

He was lost in thought until the sound of the referee's whistle brought him back to reality. The ice was cleared. A second blast of the whistle brought on the first lines. The Penguins were playing the Hawks, a team wearing white helmets and green uniforms with yellow trim. Crouched opposite Terry Mason at the face-off position was the Hawks' tall center, Phil Adams.

The whistle shrilled again. The puck was dropped. Both centers sprang into action, pounding at the small black disk with short, vicious swipes. Up on the scoreboard the seconds began ticking away. 11:59 . . . 11:58 . . . 11:57 . . .

The puck turned on end and rolled into Hawk territory. Pie, the closest to it, sprinted after it. The loose fit of his shoe-skates made him glance down at the laces. They were tight, but when he looked up again a Hawk defenseman was swooping in after the puck, stick extended far forward.

They crashed into each other, their sticks striking the puck at the same time. They fought for control of it; then Pie's skate hooked the Hawk's. He lost his balance and fell.

He looked for the puck and saw it again in the Hawks' possession. He heard his name yelled and saw Terry Mason speeding by him, his eyes smoldering.

Quickly, Pie clambered to his feet and sprinted down center ice, trying to ignore Terry's flaming look. He knew what Terry was mad about. A pass to him might have meant a score. Except for the Hawks' goalie, the space between Terry and the goal had been wide open.

A pass to a Hawk at the right of the Penguins' goal was deflected by left defenseman Frog Alexander. Frog flipped it to Chuck Billings, and a wild scramble followed as the two Hawk wingmen tried to pokecheck it away from him.

"Ice it! Ice it!" yelled Coach Joe Hayes.

The Penguins weren't able to get a clear shot at the puck, and at 10:51 the Hawks scored.

They threatened again during the next minute and almost knocked in their second goal except for a great save made by goalie Ed Courtney.

"All right, first line! Off!" yelled Coach Hayes. "Get going, second line!"

Sweat beaded Pie's forehead as he skated toward the bench. He was warm but not tired, and he wished that the coach hadn't called the line off the ice so soon.

At 7:28 Brad Krupa, right forward on the Penguins' third line, sank in a fifteen-footer to tie up the score.

The first period ended with the score still knotted, 1 to 1.

It wasn't till then that Pie thought about the twins again. He looked behind him and saw several faces he recognized, including his father's and mother's. They saw him and waved, and he waved back.

He kept searching for the other pair of familiar faces — faces that looked exactly alike — but didn't see them. Something important must have happened to keep Jody and Joliette Byrd from attending the game. Had they gone somewhere last night and not returned yet? More important, had they been home long enough to have played a game on their toy ice hockey rink?

During the second period the Hawks' Phil Adams knocked in two goals, both times assisted by one of his wingmen. The Hawks had possession of the puck most of the time, and it was only because of Ed Courtney's great saves that they were not able to drive the puck into the net more often.

With the score 3 to 1 in favor of the Hawks as the teams went into the third period, Pie Pennelli was determined to make every move count, oversize shoe-skates or not. Line 1 wasn't doing as well as the other lines up to now, and that was another reason why Terry Mason was getting hot under the collar.

Terry hadn't been doing so well himself, and Pie figured it was because the irritable center had been trying to dribble the puck to the goal and shoot it in without any help. "The terrible" Mason was disgusted with his wingmen and was trying to win the game by himself. Coach Hayes warned him about it, but after exercising caution for a minute or two, Terry started playing again as if he couldn't trust his wingmen down at their end of the rink.

It was while Line 1 was on the ice for the second time during the third period that Pie struck a Hawk's leg accidentally with his stick as he tried to pokecheck the puck and was given a minute's sentence in the penalty box for tripping. He sat there, his brows heavy with sweat, helplessly watching his teammates fight to keep the Hawks from shooting in a score.

But even Ed Courtney's fantastic moves couldn't stop them this time. It was Phil Adams again who swished the puck past him. The score was Phil's third, a hat trick. Hawks 4, Penguins 1.

Pie re-entered the game, eager to make up for lost time.

A Hawk got the pass on the face-off, passed it to a teammate, and Pie was after him as swiftly as his oversize shoeskates would allow. Just past the blue line, heading into Hawk territory, he jolted the Hawk with a neat bodycheck and stole the puck. Dribbling the black pellet with care, he swung around in a semicircle and started back across the blue line, then across the neutral zone into Penguin territory.

Two hawks charged after him and he flipped the puck to Bud. The puck rose off the ice and flopped through the air between the two Hawks, bouncing in front of Bud. Bud stopped it with his skate, then snapped it back to Pie.

Pie, heading for the right-hand side of the net, caught the puck and with one sweeping motion shoved it hard toward the narrow opening between the Hawk goalie's padded leg and the goal.

Score!

"Nice shot, Pie!" Bud cried as the wingman skated up beside him.

"Thanks, Bud."

He looked for Terry and saw the center sweeping around the net, totally ignoring him.

The meathead, thought Pie. *I scored, didn't I? He can't be mad at me for that!*

"All right, third line!" Coach Joe Hayes yelled from the bench. "Off the ice!"

"I just get going and then I have to get off," Pie grunted as he headed for the sideline.

"That's your problem," said a voice at his elbow. "You always get started too late, if you ever get started at all."

Pie glanced over his shoulder at Terry. The blue eyes met his and held unflinchingly.

"Why do you keep riding me, Mason?" Pie asked. "What have I done to you?"

"Nothing to me! It's what you're doing to the team! I don't know about you, but I'd like to get on a winning team once in my life!"

So that was it, Pie thought. Terry was blaming him for the poor direction the team was going. *But why me?* he thought. *I'm not the only one who isn't playing like a big leaguer.*

He was sure there was something else bothering Terry. Something else that made the center pick on Pie more often than he did anyone else.

Line 2 failed to score. With fifty seconds to go in the game, Line 3 banged in a twenty-footer, and the game ended with the Hawks winning, 4 to 3.

The teams skated off the ice, the Hawks triumphantly loud over their victory, the Penguins quiet and cheerless. They had learned to accept losses without crying over them. There would be other games, other chances for victory.

But one man did feel differently about losing. Terry "the terrible" Mason, who slammed down his skates on the bench and sourly left the gym.

Pie was met with a surprise greeting at the gate. The twins! He quickly forgot about Terry.

"Got a minute?" Jody whispered.

Pie stepped toward the wall with them, out of the way of the people leaving the rink.

"Didn't think you guys were here," he said. "What is it?"

Both twins looked at him as if they had something on their minds that couldn't wait another minute.

"We played a game last night and it was exactly like this one, Pie!" Jody said excitedly. "Exactly!"

Pie stared.

"Even to my getting penalized?"

"Right! Even to that!" Joliette exclaimed.

6

PIE SAT down in the locker room to take off his skates and saw Coach Hayes and Terry Mason talking together near the far wall.

Terry looked at him, and something flashed in his eyes that made Pie suspect that it was he they were talking about.

He blushed and with nervous fingers began to unlace his shoeskates. What was Terry up to now?

A few minutes later Pie left the locker room. Outside, in the bright sunshine, Bud Rooney caught up with him.

"Bud," Pie said, "what were the coach and Terry talking about?"

"You," said Bud directly.

Pie's heart skipped a beat. "That's what I figured. Did you hear what they said?"

"Not all of it," Bud replied. "But I think Terry asked to play on another line."

"What did Coach say?"

"I don't know. He didn't talk as loud as Terry did."

So, Pie thought, *the great Terry "the terrible" Mason doesn't want to play on the same line with me anymore. Suits me fine. I don't exactly enjoy playing with him either. Not with him on my back all the time.*

He couldn't guess, though, just what the coach proposed to do. He would have to wait till the next game.

That afternoon he went over to the

twins' house and found them downstairs in the recreation room, busy as beavers, drawing pollution posters.

"Our class is conducting a contest," Joliette explained enthusiastically. "The best poster on pollution wins two free tickets to a movie."

SHOW YOU CARE BY CLEARING THE AIR, read the bold heading of her poster. Underneath she had started to sketch tall smokestacks of a factory.

KILLING FISH AT SEA IS THEIR CUP OF TEA was the title of Jody's poster. Jody was sketching a weird-looking monster holding a huge cup supposedly representing an ocean. On the surface of the cup were several fish lying flat on their side, presumably dead. POLLUTION was scrawled on the monster's headdress.

Pie's jaws slackened. He had come over with hopes of playing with their toy hockey game.

"I suppose you guys won't have time to play a game of hockey since you have those posters to work on," he said.

"Oh, yes, we have!" Joliette cried, dropping her pencil. "These don't have to be in till next Thursday!"

Pie looked at her, then at Jody. He hadn't particularly considered her as his opponent. He had considered Jody.

"Well, ah . . ." he stammered, embarrassed. "Only two can play the game at the same time. Why don't you work on your poster, Jolie, while Jody and I play?"

Surprisingly, she agreed. "Okay. I understand perfectly. I'm a girl and you prefer playing with a boy. It's perfectly logical — to a boy, I guess."

66

She took up her pencil again and continued to work on the poster, showing only the least bit of disappointment.

Pie laughed. "You can play the winner," he said.

He and Jody went over to the table where the hockey game was set up, selected their sides and started to play. An old clock on a shelf beside them served as a timer.

"Three periods, twelve minutes each," Pie said. "Just like a real game."

They started to play. Within three minutes Jody scored a goal. Pie tied it up, and the game continued with each scoring twice before the period was over.

"Have you picked out yourself in the game?" Jody asked.

"That right wingman," Pie pointed. "I think he's doing better than I could, though." He paused, then said seriously, "Jody, do you really think I'll be playing like he is at our game next Saturday?"

"No," Jody said. "I think this game works only when we play it the day before the real game. That's the way it's been working out anyway."

"Then playing now doesn't mean anything?"

"I don't think so. But I'm not really sure, Pie. We can only wait and see."

"Well, if it does, playing this game might help me," Pie said, thoughtfully. "If it doesn't, at least we've had a lot of fun."

"How can it help you?" Jody asked.

"I'm slow on the ice," Pie confessed, then chuckled. "Haven't you heard Terry Mason? He broadcasts it like a radio announcer."

"Yes, I heard him." Jody scowled. "He gives me a pain."

Pie shrugged. "He's right in a lot of ways, though. I am slow, but it's not all my fault. It's my shoeskates. They're too big. They used to belong to my brother, Pat."

He didn't mind confiding that information to Jody. Jody wouldn't tell a soul.

Suddenly he saw a movement from the corner of his left eye. He turned abruptly and looked at the window above the shelf where the clock stood. The curtains were partly drawn, letting in daylight.

A face was there, and a pair of large, inquisitive eyes was staring down at them.

7

QUICKLY THE face disappeared, but not before Pie had recognized it. He looked wide-eyed at Jody.

"Did you see who that was?"

"Yes. Terry Mason." Angrily Jody ran over to the curtains and snapped them shut. "Man, he's got nerve."

"Wonder if he heard us talking."

"Probably. Did you see that grin on his face? He seemed to be getting a kick out of what he heard."

They finished the game, Pie winning by two goals. He wasn't especially pleased to play with Joliette, but he had promised her that the winner would play her and he couldn't back out.

He beat her by one point.

"You're almost better than Jody," he said frankly.

She shrugged. "Even though we're twins," she said, "I firmly think that I'm inclined to be more athletic than he is."

"Oh, sure," Jody said.

Pie thanked them for letting him play and then left. He saw Terry outside, packing snowballs and throwing them at a tree. Clinging close to his feet was his faithful cat, Tipper.

"Hi, Pie," Terry greeted, grinning. "Quite a hockey game the twins have, isn't it?"

Pie frowned. How much did Terry hear, anyway?

"What do you mean?"

"Well, it's magic, isn't it? Each player on your team represents one of us on the Penguins. Right?"

Pie let a smile curve his lips. *The best way to handle Terry Mason,* he thought, *is to agree with him.* "If you say so," he said.

"How many goals did you score? I mean *you* — not the whole team."

"Two," Pie answered.

"And I?"

"Two."

Terry scooped up a handful of snow, packed it into a firm ball and pegged it at the tree again. *Smack!* Right in the middle of its trunk.

"And you think that game will be just like the game we're playing Saturday?"

"Not necessarily."

Terry looked at him. "I thought that's what you guys said."

"You stuck your nose close enough to the window, but not your ears," Pie declared. "We said *maybe* it'll be like the game Saturday. We're not sure."

"Oh."

Terry's ears reddened as Pie, a wide grin on his face, headed for home. Let the smarty-pants believe what he wants to. He'll probably get so confused he won't know whether or not to believe that the twins' hockey game is really magic.

During the rest of the week he wondered, too, if the real game on Saturday morning would turn out to be like the one he had played with Jody. It hardly seemed likely. The last two real games were like the ones the twins had played on their toy game the Friday nights before the actual matches. It would seem that the pattern would remain the same.

On Friday afternoon, just after he had arrived home from school, there was a knock on the door. Pie answered it. It was Jody Byrd, looking as excited as if he had just seen a flying saucer.

"Hi, Pie! Coming over for a game of hockey?"

Pie considered. "I don't think I will, Jody," he confessed. "It might be like our game tomorrow, and I don't think I'd like to know beforehand how it goes. You know."

"Oh, okay. Anyway, Jolie and I have our posters done, and we made a discovery."

Pie's eyebrows arched. "What discovery?"

"We figured out what S-K-X-R-O-T

really is," Jody said proudly. "Remember Merlin the magician in the story of King Arthur?"

Pie's forehead knitted. "Yes."

"Well, in the alphabet, six letters to the right of each letter in Merlin's name spells S-K-X-R-O-T!"

Pie stared. "How'd you discover that?"

"By experimenting," Jody explained. "Jolie helped me, of course. We figured it must be a code, so we wrote the alphabet on two separate sheets of paper, then put one under the other, passing it along underneath each letter to see if S-K-X-R-O-T would spell out a word we were familiar with. Sure enough it came up with Merlin. And both of us have read about him in the King Arthur books."

"Then Merlin the magician must've been a real person," said Pie, feeling goosebumps on his arms.

76

"Must've," said Jody. "Well, see you tomorrow, Pie."

Jody left, and Pie was in the act of closing the door when he spotted a familiar figure across the street. *Terry Mason, he thought, seems to be around a lot lately when you least expect him.*

And Pie saw as he looked harder that the confused look was still on Terry's face, too.

He smiled as he closed the door.

The game at 9:00 on Saturday morning was against the Seals, a team wearing blue uniforms with white trim. As he skated around the ice to warm up for the game, Pie looked at the stands for the familiar faces of the twins. He saw them finally, waved, and they waved back.

Wonder how their game turned out? he thought. *And I wonder how I played?*

He pushed the thoughts out of his mind

as a skater whisked past him, spun half way around and skated backward, facing him. Their eyes met and held. This time not even a flicker of a smile spoiled the wax-like features of Terry's face.

Near the corner of the rink Terry spun half way around again and continued skating frontward. *He's baffled,* Pie thought. *He doesn't believe in magic, so he doesn't know what to think about me, the twins, or their toy hockey game.*

Now that I've got him guessing maybe he'll lay off me, Pie thought. *But I'd better not count on it.*

Face-off time rolled around, and the first lines of both teams got in position on the ice. Terry centered against Corky Jones, a boy shorter than Terry, but muscular and fast.

The whistle shrilled, the puck was dropped, and the centers' sticks clattered against the ice for possession of the puck. The rubber disk took a severe battering, then skittered across the ice into Penguin territory. Bud Rooney hooked it with the blade of his stick, whisked around, and started back up the ice. Pie, moving slowly in the neutral zone toward his own blue line, waited for the puck to cross into Seal territory.

Challenged by a Seal who came upon him suddenly from behind, Bud snapped the puck. Pie sprinted across the blue line in an effort to get in front of it, and *shreek!* the whistle pulled him up short.

"You were off side, Pennelli!" Terry yelled.

Pie blushed. That was stupid, he admitted. He had misjudged the speed of the puck and had caused a violation by crossing the blue line before the puck had.

The face-off was at the Penguin end of the rink between Frog and a Seal wingman. The Seal got control of the puck, passed it to another Seal, who caught it and bolted for the Penguin net. Pie lunged forward, sprinting as hard as he could to get between the goal and the oncoming Seal.

Suddenly his left skate twisted and his ankle gave way, throwing him off balance. He fell, skidded on the ice, and a player in a black uniform toppled over him.

A storming "You idiot!" identified the skater. It was Terry.

Terry clambered to his feet, his eyes blazing hot. Behind him a cry of jubilation had exploded, and Pie could see sticks rising in the air like spears as the Seals celebrated their first goal.

"I'm sorry," Pie apologized. "My ankle gave way."

"Your ankle!" Terry scoffed. "You know what's the matter with you? You haven't learned how to keep your balance yet, and you're trying to cut corners going eighty miles an hour! Well, you can't do that, Pie! You have to learn to keep your balance first!"

"C'mon, you guys!" yelled Coach Hayes. "Off the ice!"

Line 1 skated off and Line 2 skated on. Pie, tired and sweaty, avoided the coach's eyes as he climbed over the wall and sat down. *Terry had no business talking to me like that,* he thought. *Not on the ice in front of all that crowd. Not anywhere.*

One of these days I'm going to surprise him, Pie promised himself. I'll break every one of his teeth.

The fault was in his shoeskates, of course. *But if I told that to Terry,* Pie thought, *he'd laugh and say that that ex-*

81

cuse was worse than none.

He watched Line 2 and then Line 3 do their stuff, and helped in the cheering when Butch Morrison, Line 3's center for the Penguins, knocked in a goal to knot the score.

Back on the ice went Line 1, and this time Pie tried his best not to cut corners sharply and risk a spill. But after awhile he realized that he might as well have stayed off the ice as stick rigidly to that rule. Playing hockey *was* skating as fast as you could, stopping quickly as you could, and cutting corners as sharply as possible. There was no other way to play the game and play it well. Fall or not, that was the way he was going to play it.

Terry, he told himself, could lump it.

An offside violation was called on Chuck Billings. And on the face-off in neutral territory Bud got the pass and shot it to Terry. Terry dribbled the puck up the ice, across the blue line and into Seals' territory. He was suddenly trapped by two Seals who came swooping down at him from different directions.

He tried to pass the puck between them to Bud Rooney, but one of the Seals stopped it with his skate. The puck skidded to the side and Pie, speeding down the ice near the boards, cut in and snared it. Pulling the puck safely toward him, he put on a burst of speed and carried it down the ice toward the Seals' goal.

From ten feet away he shot.

A save!

"Why didn't you pass it, Pie?" Bud Rooney cried.

There, on the other side of the crease,

Pie saw the wingman in the open.

Pie skated around the back of the net, coming up behind Bud. "Sorry, Bud," he said.

"Sure," Bud grumbled.

"Come on, you guys! Move! Move!" yelled Coach Hayes.

Too late both Pie and Bud saw the fast breakaway the Seals had made. Two of them had the puck up the ice, and the only Penguin on their tails was Terry Mason.

A quick pass to the wingman on the left, then a pass back to the wingman on the right. Then — *snap!*

Goal!

Pie slowed down as he reached the net, and as the center made a sharp turn in front of the crease and skated up to him, Pie found himself face to face with Terry.

"If you want to rest why don't you get off the ice?" Terry growled. "Those guys had the puck halfway up the ice while you were still yakking with Bud."

"I just told him that I was sorry I didn't pass to him," said Pie. "What's wrong with that?"

Thirty seconds later a Seal stole the puck from Pie, sped alone down the ice, and belted it past Ed Courtney's left shoulder for a goal.

Pie looked on, stunned.

8

"OFF THE ICE!" yelled the coach. "Pronto!"

Pie sprinted off, pulled up sharply near the boards, and stepped over the wall. As the other members of Line 1 skated off the ice, Line 2 scrambled on.

"That Seal surprise you, Pie?" Coach Hayes asked, smiling.

Pie, his chest heaving with each inhaled breath, nodded. He expected a lecture from the coach about the play, but Coach Hayes said nothing more.

There was nothing to say, anyway, Pie

thought. *The Seal just stole that puck from me and took off. That's all there was to it. The guy was just lucky he had open ice ahead of him. A thing like that doesn't happen often.*

And it's a good thing it doesn't, Pie thought grimly.

The teams' third lines scrambled onto the ice and then off again without scoring.

"Let's have some teamwork this period," Coach Hayes prompted as Line 1 got on the ice to start off the second period. "Terry, quit yelling at Pie out there or you might be watching the rest of the game from the bench."

"Who's yelling at him?" Terry snorted and zipped onto the ice without waiting for a reply.

The men skated to their positions. The face-off. The fight to control the puck.

Bang! Terry socked it to Bud. Bud dribbled it into Seal territory and was suddenly bodychecked, but not before he drove the puck against the boards. It bounced back onto the ice and skittered toward the Seals' goal where Pie and the two Seals' defensemen charged after it. Pie, feeling his oversize shoeskates hampering his speed, kicked the ice accidentally with the toe of his skate and fell flat on his stomach.

The Seals got the puck, passed it back up the ice and shot it to a wingman. Pie felt a hand grab his arm and help him to his feet.

He didn't see who his benefactor was until the guy had sped away on his skates. It was Terry.

Pie bolted after him, ignoring the powdery ice that covered the entire front of his uniform. He sped alongside the boards, this time trying not to stumble. It would be awful if Terry had to pick him up again.

Frog Alexander stole the puck away from a Seal and belted it up the ice to Terry. Terry swerved in a half circle, the puck hooked in the curve of the blade of his stick, and started back up the ice with it. Two Seals charged after him from his left and right sides, and he passed to Pie.

Pie stickhandled the puck across the blue line, then across the neutral zone into Seal territory. Now the Seals' defensemen were after him, arms and legs churning as they swept upon him like vultures. Far ahead he saw the Seals' goalie crouched in front of the net, wide open spaces around him.

Pie glanced at the puck — taking just enough time to make certain that the blade of his stick would strike it exactly right — and swung.

Smack! The puck lifted off the ice and sailed through the air like a miniature flying saucer. It headed for the upper right-hand corner of the net, just over the goalie's left shoulder. The goalie reached for it, and for a second his huge glove obscured the flying missile. It looked as if he had caught the puck, and Pie's heart sank.

Then he heard the exploding yell from the fans, and saw the goalie's arm dropping, and there in the corner of the net was the black disk falling to the ice.

"Nice shot, Pie!" Bud yelled, slapping him on the shoulder.

From the bench came the resounding thunder of Penguin sticks banging against the boards.

"All right, Line 1!" Coach Hayes

91

shouted. "Off the ice! Line 2, take over! *Do* something!"

Pie took his time skating off. His legs ached. His body was hot and sweaty. *I could go for a shower right now,* he thought.

"Nice shooting, Pie," Coach Hayes praised him as he stepped through the gate and sat down. "It was perfect."

He looked at the scoreboard. HOME 3, VISITORS 2. The VISITORS were the Penguins.

Line 2 held the Seals. Then Line 3 scored, tieing it up.

It was still 3 to 3 when the second period ended.

As Pie waited for the whistle that would signal the first lines to get back on the ice for the start of the third period, someone touched him on the shoulder.

92

"Pie!" a voice whispered into his ear.

He looked around. It was Jody Byrd, looking wide-eyed as ever.

"Yeah, what?" Pie asked.

Jody hesitated. "I don't know whether I should tell you this," he said reluctantly.

"Tell me what?" asked Pie.

"This last period is going to be bad," Jody replied. "Real bad."

Pie looked him straight in the eyes. "I'm sorry you told me," he said.

9

THE WHISTLE blew for the start of the third period, and Pie went onto the ice, his knees feeling like rubber.

He skated to his position opposite the Seals' wing and carefully watched the puck as the referee dropped it and the centers fought for its control. The pellet shot on edge toward the left side of the rink where both Bud Rooney and a Seals' defenseman pounced on it with their sticks.

Then the Seal whacked it against the boards. Pie, quickly determining where he might intercept the puck, sprinted to the spot as the rubber pellet bounced back. He hooked it with the blade of his stick and charged up the ice, skating parallel with the boards, stickhandling the puck with perfect ease. But his legs felt weak, and he knew he wasn't skating as fast as he normally could.

A Seal defenseman bolted up behind him and whisked the puck away from him before he realized what happened. Back up the ice the Seal swept the puck in the opposite direction. Pie watched, half stunned.

"C'mon, Pie!" Terry yelled. "Look alive!"

Pie pulled himself together and sprinted after the puck. He saw the Seal pass to a wingman who had swept in from the left side of the net. A quick snap

96

sent the puck flying past Ed Courtney before the goalie could lift his arm. A goal!

Pie, head bowed, slowed down, turned, and coasted toward his position. He was bone-tired, and he dreaded the thought that he had to come onto the ice once again after this session.

"C'mon, Pie. Wake up," Terry said as he skated up beside the weary wingman. "If you're tired, why don't you get off the ice? Let somebody else take over."

Pie wanted to do that desperately, but he wouldn't go voluntarily. He preferred to have the coach call him off. It wouldn't look so bad if Coach Hayes yanked him.

The whistle shrilled, sending a shock wave through his head that made him squinch.

The face-off. Suddenly he saw the puck

skittering past his left skate. He caught it with his stick and carried it swiftly across the blue line and then the red line into Seal territory. A Seal charged at him. He saw no one to pass to, so he shot the puck against the boards. Then he bolted forward to catch the rebound. But a Seal defenseman reached it first and belted it across the ice to a wingman. Two passes and the puck was down near the Penguin goal. Ed Courtney was protecting the net with all the ability and agility he had, but he didn't have enough of either one.

The puck sailed past his padded left leg for the Seals' fifth goal.

The first lines went off the ice, replaced by the second lines, and Pie sat on the bench, his chest heaving.

"You're bushed, Pie," the coach said. "Didn't you get enough rest last night?"

Pie shrugged. He didn't answer.

The Penguins' second line had control of the puck during most of the time they were on the ice, but the Seals' goaltender matched every shot made at the net. He had five saves before the lines skated off the ice and the third lines skated on.

At 6:23 Butch Morrison, the Penguins' center for Line 3, scored, bringing them up within a goal of the leading Seals, 5 to 4.

Terry looked at Pie as they skated toward their positions.

"I suppose you're playing this last time because of that toy hockey game," Terry said.

Pie glanced at him. "What do you mean by that?"

Terry's lips curved in a half smile. "You know what I mean. That toy hockey game the Byrd twins found in their attic is supposed to be magic, isn't it?"

"Oh." Pie shrugged. "Yeah. I suppose it is. Real genuine magic."

They skated past the center spot and were heading for the right forward position, yet Terry had made no attempt to stop.

"So now you're sure you know our secret," Pie said, stopping at his position. Terry remained silent, and Pie knew that the center was only guessing. Terry really wasn't sure whether or not to believe Pie about the toy hockey game's being endowed with magical powers.

The whistle shrilled. "C'mon, Terry," the ref snapped. "Let's go."

Terry shot Pie a final questioning look, then skated to his position at center. A trace of a smile flickered over Pie's face.

The ref dropped the puck, and the clock started up again for Line 1's last time on the ice. *Maybe Terry was still thinking of the toy hockey game,* Pie thought, *because Corky Jones, the Seals' center, got the drop on him.* He slapped the puck away, sprinted after it himself, then shot it to a wingman heading up the ice alongside the boards.

Pie bolted down the rink on the opposite side, staying in the clear in case either Bud or Frog managed to intercept the puck. Near the corner Frog bodychecked the speeding Seal wingman, who passed the puck to a teammate sprinting up center ice toward the Penguins' goal.

Slap! A beautiful drive directly at the net! Ed Courtney got in front of it and stopped it expertly with his padded chest. A save. The puck dropped in front of him, and he covered it with his glove.

The whistle blew. Calmly, Ed picked up the puck and tossed it to the ref.

Again the face-off, and the black pellet

skittered to Pie. He pushed it gently ahead of him, heading toward the right corner of the Seals' net.

At the back of his mind echoed Jody Byrd's whispered warning. *This last period is going to be bad. Real bad.*

How bad could it be? Pie wondered.

Suddenly blue and white uniforms converged on him, with sticks looking like the tentacles of a ruffled octopus. Pie glanced quickly behind and saw both Bud and Terry approaching from the other side of the net, waiting for him to pass.

He struck the puck. It hit the skate of one of the Seals and bounced back, and he found himself scrambling for it with the two Seals. His face was hot and his arms and legs felt like iron weights.

Suddenly his vision got hazy. His head

swam, and his legs became like jelly. Someone collided into him and down he went, hitting the ice hard. He lay there in a sea of blackness, while far away a whistle shrilled in short, sharp blasts.

He was tired and sleepy. So tired and sleepy.

After a while his head cleared. His vision became normal, and he heard Coach Hayes' voice. "Feel better, Pie? Can you get up?"

He nodded, and the coach helped him to his feet and off the ice.

It wasn't until he was sitting on the bench that he noticed a Seal sitting in the penalty box across the rink.

"What's he in for?" Pie asked.

"Illegal bodychecking," Coach Hayes said.

"On me?"

"Yes."

Pie frowned. "But it wasn't his fault. It was mine. I've been bushed. Real bushed. I — I just passed out, that's all."

"That's what I thought, too," Coach Hayes said. "I shouldn't have let you go out there this last time."

He watched the rest of the game from the bench. There was no more scoring, and the Seals won, 5 to 4.

The Byrd twins met Pie outside and walked home with him. Pie noticed that Terry was trailing behind them, trying to get within earshot of what they were saying. He warned them not to say anything about the toy hockey game until Terry was gone.

"Well, did the game come out like the toy game did?" he asked, when Terry was no longer trailing.

"It sure did," Jody said. "Except that we didn't know what happened to you in our game. Our hockey players don't get knocked down, you know!"

Pie laughed. "How did that part show up in your game?"

"Simple. You and two Seals kept scrambling for the puck. Suddenly you stopped moving."

"I did?"

"Yes. Just long enough for Jolie — I mean one of the Seals — to grab the puck and pass it on."

"But why did I stop moving? Or how?" Pie wanted to know, staring wide-eyed from one twin to the other.

Jody shrugged. "You just jammed, that's all. You didn't move." His cheeks dimpled. "I suppose that's when you were knocked out!"

Pie grinned. "I suppose," he said.

He saw the twins off and on during the next few days. But it wasn't until Friday that Jody called and told him some shocking news.

"Something's happened to our hockey game, Pie! Jolie and I looked high and low for it, but we can't find it anywhere!"

Pie frowned. "You have no idea what's happened to it?" he asked.

"No! We just know it's missing!"

10

PIE WENT over to the twins' house to help look for the game. Immediately he noticed a difference in the basement from the last time he had visited it. The tiled floor was polished and the furniture dusted. Something else seemed different about it, but he couldn't quite figure out what it was.

"Has the furniture been changed around?" he asked the twins. "Something looks different."

"Dad moved the sofa from that wall to that one," Joliette explained, pointing to a paneled wall and then to the sofa underneath the basement window.

A look at the window drew a double-take from Pie.

"I don't remember seeing that window open before," he said.

"Dad must've opened it when he cleaned here last night," Jody said. "He does that to air the basement out."

"No one could've come in through there, if that's what you're thinking," said Joliette. "There's a screen behind it. Anyway, who would do a thing like that?"

"Terry 'the terrible' Mason, maybe?" Jody said, his eyebrows arching as he glanced at Pie.

Pie shrugged. "Well, we saw him peeking in that window. He knows where you kept the game."

He looked at the table at the far side

of the room on which the twins had kept the game always ready for play. The regular four chairs were grouped around it.

"Are you sure your father didn't put it somewhere?"

"Why should he?" Jody said. "He knows that Jolie and I play with it a lot."

"Have you asked him?"

"He isn't home. He won't be till tomorrow afternoon," replied Jody.

"He's a salesman," Joliette explained.

"I suppose you've asked your mother about it?"

"Of course," Joliette replied. "But she doesn't know a thing about it."

Pie sighed. "I wonder how that'll affect tomorrow's game."

"Why should it?" Joliette asked.

"It always did before," said Pie. A thought occurred to him. "I wonder what

111

would happen if Terry had taken it," he said. "Up till now he isn't sure whether it has magical powers or not. He's just been guessing. Maybe he wants to experiment with it."

"Think it'll work for him?" Jody said.

"Why not? It's magic. The power is in the game, isn't it? Not in the people who play it."

He went out and paused on the curb of the sun-drenched street. There, beside the tree where Pie had seen him once before, stood Terry Mason. Smiling. At his feet was his favorite companion, Tipper.

Pie braced himself.

"Terry," he said, "have you got the twins' hockey game?"

Terry stared at him. "The twins' hockey game?" he echoed. The smile vanished. "What would I want with their old hockey game?"

"It's missing," Pie said.

Terry's fists clenched as he came at Pie. "Are you accusing me of stealing it, Pie-face?"

Pie stood his ground. "We saw you looking through the window the other night," he said defiantly.

"That doesn't mean I stole it!" Terry snapped. "Maybe it disappeared by itself. It *was* magic, wasn't it?" A laugh of mockery tore from his lips.

Pie matched his glaring eyes, not certain whether to believe him or not. "See you at the rink," he said.

He felt a rubbing against his leg, looked down and saw Tipper looking up at him, eyes like large yellow marbles.

"Hi, Tipper," Pie said, smiling.

"*Meow!*" Tipper said.

Terry picked it up. "C'mon, Tip," he said, walking away, "before he starts ask-

ing *you* questions about that dumb hockey game."

Pie lay in bed that night thinking about the missing game. What could have happened to it, anyway? Had someone really stolen it from the basement, or had Mr. Byrd put it somewhere where the twins were unable to find it? Or, as Terry had suggested, had it disappeared? Did the game really possess such magical powers that it *could* disappear by itself?

It was a long time before sleep finally overtook him.

The next morning, as he was putting on his uniform to prepare for the game against the Bears, he heard the distant ring of the telephone and a few moments later his mother's voice, "Pie! Never mind getting dressed!"

He froze and stared at the door. Then

he went to it and shouted down the hall, "Mom! What did you say?"

"Coach Hayes just called," she said from the bottom of the stairs. "He said that the game's called off."

He stared, shivers rippling up his spine. "Did he say why, Mom?"

"The electric power's off," she explained. "The game is postponed till some future date."

11

AFTER BREAKFAST Pie went over to the Byrds' house and told the twins the sad news. Their eyes popped. Their mouths sagged open.

"Isn't that something?" Jody whispered tensely.

"That toy hockey game has more magical powers than I realized!" Joliette exclaimed in the same breathless whisper. "It's fantastic!"

"Fantastic is right," replied Pie, keeping his voice down too so as not to let Mrs. Byrd hear. No telling what she might say if she heard them discussing magical powers. "I've talked with Terry Mason about it. I practically accused him of stealing the game."

"What did he say?" Joliette asked.

"He said he didn't steal it. And was he mad!"

"Do you think he did?" Jody inquired.

"I don't think so. He wouldn't have gotten so sore if he had. I was sorry afterwards that I accused him. It was a dumb thing to do, since I was only guessing, anyway."

"Yeah, that's right," said Jody. "Well, it's going to be a dull day now that the hockey game was called off. Wonder what will happen if we never find our hockey game?"

"Good question," said Pie.

Joliette shivered. "We've got to find it,"

she said. "I won't ever sleep again if we don't."

It wasn't a dull day for Pie. His father started to build a partition in the basement to make a carpenter shop for himself, and Pie helped him. Working got his mind off the missing toy hockey game. But when they finished for the day his thoughts reverted back to it.

What effect would there be on the real hockey rink if the toy hockey game could never be found again?

It was something to worry about.

At five minutes of eight that night Jody called. His voice was bubbling with excitement.

"We've found the hockey game, Pie!" he cried.

Pie's heart skipped a beat. "Where was it?"

"Dad had put it on a shelf in the basement and then covered it with an old rug! Unintentionally!"

A wave of relief swept over Pie. "That's the best news I've heard in years, Jody," he said. "Well, there's something I must do now, for sure."

"What?" Jody asked.

"Apologize to Terry," Pie replied. "And I can think of a million things I'd rather do than that!"

"I know what you mean," Jody said. "But I suppose it's best. It'll rest on your conscience if you don't."

"Right," said Pie. "Well, thanks for the good news, Jody. See you."

"How about coming over next Friday night and playing a game?"

"Okay! See you then."

It was after church on Sunday morning

when Pie met Terry and considered apologizing to him. But their parents were around, and Pie couldn't gather up enough nerve.

Later that day, when he was returning from the gorge after a look at the ice-caked falls, he met Terry again. Terry had his cat with him, trailing at his heels.

"Terry, I — I want to see you a minute," Pie said. His heart was thumping. He'd rather jump into ice-cold water than apologize to Terry Mason. But, as Jody Byrd had said, the guilt would rest on his conscience if he didn't.

"That's a switch," Terry said.

"I owe you an apology," Pie said. "I accused you of stealing that hockey game from the Byrd twins, and I'm sorry."

"Why? Did they find it?"

"Yes. Mr. Byrd had stuck it up on a

shelf, then covered it with an old rug." The thumping began to disappear. "Well, that's all I wanted to say."

Terry looked at him a long minute. "Okay," he said at last.

They passed by each other and continued on their way. Suddenly Terry yelled, "Pie?"

Pie looked around. "Yes?"

Terry was holding his cat. "Thanks!"

"Sure," said Pie.

There was an item in the *Deep Gorge News* Monday evening about the electric power system's being repaired at Davis Rink and that the game between the Penguins and the Hawks would be played as scheduled. The Penguins–Bears game, which was called off last Saturday morning due to the power's being off, would be played sometime in January

On Friday night Pie went over to the

twins' house again. After visiting for a while with Mr. and Mrs. Byrd, he and the twins descended to the basement, sat at the table in front of the toy hockey game, chose their teams and started to play. Since tomorrow's game was with the Hawks, Jody called his team the Hawks and Pie called his the Penguins. Joliette kept time and the score.

The game started with the usual face-off at center. Jody's man grabbed the puck, zipped down the rink and *swish!* A shot that missed the goal by a hair.

The puck bounced off the corner and into the rink, and Pie raced after it with a defensive player. The player brought the puck up the ice, shot it across the blue line, and a Penguin wingman stopped it.

"That's you, Pie!" Joliette cried excitedly.

So it was, Pie realized. He moved the

man up the ice, and *snap!* The man spun and the puck shot off the edge of his stick. Missed!

The puck whipped around the corner. Jody's man intercepted it, shot, and again Pie caught it.

Slap! A close one! But again a miss.

One of Jody's men grabbed the puck, carried it up the ice and shot. Goal!

"Sorry about that," Jody said, grinning.

In the second period Pie tried his best to tie up the score, but his shots kept missing by slim margins. Then he tried a new tack. He passed to another player, not realizing who it was until the player scored and Joliette shouted, "That man's Terry, Pie!"

The fast action continued, and Pie found himself sweating. He blamed it on the excitement and the action, but he knew that the real reason for it was knowing that the game was a preview of tomorrow's real game.

Almost halfway through the second period the man who represented him passed to the man representing Terry, and again the man scored.

"You're ahead, Pie!" Joliette shouted.

Pie smiled. Perhaps that was the smart thing to do — keep passing to Terry, regardless of how they felt toward each other. Playing the best together was the way to play the game.

Then, about a minute later, Pie's right wing failed to budge when Pie twisted the control lever. He twisted it this way and that, but the figure remained almost stationary.

That's me again, he realized, staring. *Would that mean disaster in the real game?* A chill ran down his spine.

12

TIME!" PIE called, and Joliette wrote down the time on a notepad.

Pie tried to lift the hockey figure off the metal rod that projected straight up out of the slot about an inch, and it slid off easily.

"It's gotten loose," Jody observed.

"Twisting it so many times must've loosened it," Pie reasoned. "Those little staples in the wood came out just enough to lose their hold on the rod."

There were two such staples driven into the hockey figure, square ones to fit over the square rods. He put the hockey

127

figure back in place, fitted the staples over the rod, then tried to force the staples further into the wood with his thumb. He couldn't.

"Get me something to tap them with," he said.

Jody produced a hammer from a wall laden with tools and handed it to him. A light tap on each staple made the hockey figure secure again. Pie twisted the controls back and forth, and the figure whipped this way and that like new.

"Well, I'm in shape again," he said happily. "But it's funny why that happened to *me*. The man representing me, I mean."

"I thought of that," said Jody. "Think it really means something, Pie?"

"I don't know. I won't know till we play tomorrow."

"In my opinion it definitely means

something," Joliette said with conviction. "I don't know what and I don't think it's serious, because you're back in the game. But I bet it means *something*."

"But those staples coming loose could be just an accident," Pie said.

"No accident," Jody said, as he jiggled the other figures on their rods. "Look. Every one of them is tight. Why should the staples only on yours come loose?"

Pie inhaled deeply and emptied his lungs with a long, drawn-out sigh. "That's right," he said. "Why?"

"Let's finish the game," Jody suggested. "Let's see what else is going to happen tomorrow."

"You two finish it," Pie said, feeling a tension mounting inside him. "I don't think I'd care to know what else is going to happen to me tomorrow."

He left the table.

"Maybe that's what it meant!" Joliette cried. "You'll be leaving the game!"

"For good?" Her brother wrinkled his nose. "Nuts, Jolie. That's only the second period. What *might* happen is that Pie will go out for a while for some reason *other* than a normal one, and then go back in again."

"You could've let me finish," Joliette said, glaring at him.

"Sorry. Sure you don't want to finish the game, Pie?"

"I'm sure," said Pie. "See you tomorrow — after the game."

The rest of the evening — from the time he left the twins till he went to bed — dragged like a snail crossing the Mojave Desert. So did the morning — from the time he got up till the time he went to the

131

game. What *did* that accident in the toy hockey game mean, anyway?

The buzzer sounded for the start of the game and the Line 1 players of both the Hawks and the Penguins skated to their positions. The whistle shrilled.

Face-off!

Phil Adams, the Hawks' center, knocked the puck to his left wingman. The man scooted down the length of the ice close to the boards, then cut in sharply toward the Penguins' net. Just as Frog Alexander swooped toward him, his stick outstretched to pokecheck the puck, the Hawk shot. Like a missile the black pellet flew through the air toward the net — and missed by inches!

The puck bounced off the wall behind the net, Pie after it. The defensive Hawk beside him reached the puck first, and

Pie bumped into him. He tried to hold his balance as he scrambled to pokecheck the puck, but his oversize shoeskates prevented him from shifting around as quickly as he wanted to. In a second he found himself sprawled on the ice while the Hawk defenseman dribbled the puck toward Penguin territory.

"Come on, Pie!" yelled a familiar voice. "On your feet!"

He scrambled up, ignoring Terry Mason's commanding yell. Apparently apologizing to Terry for accusing him of stealing the Byrd twins' toy hockey game hadn't changed his attitude a bit.

Pie saw the Hawk defenseman glancing at a wing, and sprinted up the ice. Just as Frog and Terry met the oncoming Hawk, the man snapped a pass to the wing.

Anticipating the play, Pie bolted forward, stretched out his stick, and intercepted the pass. He sprinted for the net. Ten feet from it he shot. The puck sailed through the air. Up went the Hawk goalie's hand. A save!

A minute later Pie accepted a pass from Frog, shot, and again the Hawk goalie's gloved hand picked it out of the air like a frog's quick tongue catching a fly.

Oh, man! Pie thought disappointedly. *I can't get one through him!*

The face-off. Then a Hawk was dribbling the puck up the ice, stickhandling it as if the pellet was magnetized to his stick. My man! Pie realized, and sprinted after him.

The Hawk swept by Frog, weaved around Chuck and reached the side of

134

the Penguins' net. *Snap!* There were only inches between Ed Courtney's padded legs and the side of the net, but the puck sailed through for a Hawks' score.

"That was your man, Pie!" Terry snapped as the first line skated off the ice and the second line skated on.

"I can see," Pie replied indignantly. "But these skates are — "

He caught himself and met Terry's flashing eyes.

"Skates are what?" Terry asked, smiling. "Too small? Too big? I was wondering when you were going to blame *something*."

"Fact is, they are big," Pie said as they climbed over the wall and sat down. "They belonged to my brother. And his feet are bigger than mine. Lots bigger."

Terry's lips parted as if he were going

135

to say something, then closed again. The reaction surprised Pie. It wasn't like Terry to shut up like a clam. *Something that I said,* Pie thought, *had made him change his mind.*

What?

Pie remembered that Bob, Terry's older brother and a former hockey player here at Deep Gorge, was also attending State College. "What do you hear from Bob?" he asked, hoping that a little dialogue might help Terry forget his differences with him.

"Nothing," Terry said.

"He's playing, isn't he?"

"Yeah. Yeah, sure."

He didn't seem to want to talk any more about Bob, and Pie didn't push him. But it sure was funny how he had clammed up so fast.

136

The score remained 1 to 0 going into the second period. Line 1 was back on the ice. This is the period, Pie thought — a shiver racing up his spine — when something is supposed to happen to me.

But after a few moments on the ice he forgot the incident, forgot last night, forgot everything except what was happening now.

Twice he took shots at the goal and missed. Each time he expected a yell from Terry, but the center was keeping silent. Pie couldn't believe it. Had mentioning Pat's skates to him really made that much difference?

A Hawk was dribbling the puck past Pie. Pie sped after him, bodychecked him near the defensive blue line, grabbed the puck and bolted up the ice with it. Ten feet from the Hawks' net he met the oncoming Hawk defensemen and considered taking a shot. Suddenly he saw one of his own men skating in from the left side of the net. It was Terry. Instinctively, Pie shot the puck to him. Terry caught it, and *snap!* Into the net for a goal!

Terry glided by Pie, and was instantly smothered by the other Penguins. "Nice going, Terry!" "Great shot, man!" they shouted.

Pie skated around the net, a spark of pride kindled in his heart. Terry was getting the praises, but it was Pie who had passed him the puck. And an assist, like a score, counted as a point, too.

The clock was ticking off the seconds toward the ten-minute mark when Pie intercepted a Hawk rebound off the boards and sprinted down center ice with it. As Pie breezed over the blue line into Hawk territory, a Hawk rammed into him with a neat bodycheck and knocked him down. The Hawk wingman quickly stretched out his stick, hooked its blade around the puck, and yanked it toward him.

Scrambling to his feet, Pie maneuvered himself between the Hawk and the puck, then shifted quickly and sped around the Hawk toward the opponents' net. The rink was open in front of him, and he was about to swat the puck for a shot at the goal, when both the goalie and a Hawk defenseman got in the line of fire.

Just then Pie saw a Penguin sweeping in from the left. It was Terry. Pie snapped the puck to him. The pass was perfect. Terry stopped it, and with a quick snap, scored.

Again Terry received the plaudits from his teammates. This time he skated up to

Pie, puffing hard. "Thanks, Pie," he said. "And also for the first one."

Pie, dead tired, only smiled.

"Nice passwork, Pie," Coach Hayes said to him as Line 1 came off the ice and Line 2 went on. "By the way, I heard you asking Terry about his brother, Bob."

"Yes."

"Did you know that Bob didn't make the team?"

Pie stared. "No, I didn't."

"Of course Pat did and is doing real well," said the coach. "Come to think of it, Pie, maybe that's why Terry's been bugging you. He's hurt that Bob isn't playing and Pat is, and has been taking it out on you."

Like a bombshell Pie realized the logic of that reasoning. Terry was a kid who would do exactly that.

"That must be it, Coach," he said. "It can't be anything else."

Line 2 couldn't score, but they held the Hawks from scoring, too. Line 3 did well until 6:23, when a Hawk drove in a shot to tie up the score, 2 to 2.

Meanwhile, Pie rested and tried to remember what had happened in the game he had played with Jody Byrd last night. But he was so tired he gave up.

Coach Hayes' yell, "Okay, Line 1, on the ice!" came ever too quickly.

The Hawks grabbed the puck from face-off and worked it toward the Penguins' goal with expert stickhandling before Frog managed to steal it and drive it back up the ice. Just before it reached the blue line, and to prevent an icing charge, Pie snared it. He started to dribble it through the neutral zone into

Hawk territory when a man bumped into him with a hard bodycheck and sent him sprawling.

Pie clambered to his feet and a sudden discovery reeled him. Something was wrong with his right skate!

He looked and his heart sank.

The front part of the skate had broken loose from the shoe!

13

PIE LEFT the ice, bone-tired and sick at heart. He'd have to watch the rest of the game from the bench, but what about afterward? Was he finished with skating? Would his father buy him a new pair?

The coach sent Jim Stanton in to replace him. Jim was a wing on Line 2.

"Too bad, Pie," Coach Hayes said. "But those skates looked too big for you in the first place. Were they?"

Pie nodded.

"Thought so. Skates should fit tighter than your regular shoes," Coach Hayes advised. "When you get your new pair, make sure they're a tight fit." He grinned and squeezed Pie's knee. "You'll find that you'll skate a lot better."

Seconds later someone tapped him on the shoulder. He looked around. It was Jody.

"That's what that trouble meant!" Jody whispered.

Pie frowned. "What trouble?"

Suddenly he knew what Jody was referring to. The hockey figure representing him on the toy hockey game coming loose on the rod last night! It had forecast today's incident as closely as anything possibly could!

"That's right!" Pie said breathlessly. "That's really right! And it happened in the second period, too! Just like it did here!"

146

Just then laughter exploded from the fans, and a whistle shrilled.

"Hey, look!" Jody shouted, pointing.

Pie looked, and there on the ice — running and slipping and sliding on its haunches near the Hawks' goal — was a calico cat!

"It's Tipper! Terry's cat!"

"Tipper!" Terry shouted and skated after it. He scooped it up and carried it gingerly to a little, blond-haired girl behind the boards. The girl, Pie saw, was Terry's sister, Pam.

The laughter changed to applause as Pam sat down with the cat on her lap, and Terry returned to the ice, shaking his head and smiling.

The game resumed. Seconds before Line 1 left the ice Terry knocked in his third score of the game with an assist by

Jim Stanton, the kid who had replaced Pie.

"A hat trick!" Pie cried, applauding. "Nice shot, Terry! Nice pass, Jim!"

"Thought you didn't like him," Jody said from behind him.

Pie shrugged. "Oh, he's really not as terrible as he pretends to be."

The game went into the third period, and finally ended, 3 to 2, in the Penguins' favor. Terry Mason had scored every goal for the Penguins.

As Pie was leaving the rink with the twins, Terry ran up beside them, grinning broadly and proudly. At his heels was Pam, carrying Tipper.

"Hi," he said.

"Hi," they greeted him.

"Going to play with your hockey game this afternoon?"

The twins looked at Pie, their eyes carrying a secret message. "Shall we, Pie?"

Pie shrugged. "Why not?"

Terry chuckled. "I wonder if . . . well, mind if I came over and played, too?"

Again the twins and Pie exchanged a look. Then Pie winked.

"Of course, you know why he wants to come over and play, don't you?" he said.

"Of course," said Jody. "He wants to see whether the game is really magic."

"Right. Okay, Terry. If it's all right with the twins, it's all right with me."

"Oh, it's all right with us!" replied the twins.

"Thanks!" said Terry, his teeth flashing white as he grinned. "See you guys later! Oh, one more thing. Sorry about your skate, Pie. I hope you'll get a new pair."

"Me, too," Pie replied.

He really wasn't surprised when his father saw the broken skate and said, "No doubt about it now, son. You've got to have a new pair. We'll go to a store together after lunch."

At 1:00 they walked to a store and Mr. Pennelli bought Pie a new pair of skates, one that fit tighter than his regular shoes. Pie was sure that he would never again make a quick turn with his feet moving before his skates did.

At 3:00 Terry showed up at the twins' house. They called Pie over, and all four of them went down to the basement. Terry had his cat with him, which didn't surprise Pie. Those two were practically inseparable.

They reached the table on which the hockey game was set and started to sit down, when suddenly the cat cried, "*Meow!*" and leaped off Terry's shoulder directly onto the game.

He sat there, gazing big-eyed at the miniature hockey figures, until Terry yelled, "Git, Tipper! Where are your manners?"

The cat jumped off.

At the same time something clicked in Pie's mind as he stared at the cat. He looked at the twins, and from their expressions he knew that the same thing had clicked in their minds, too.

Beware what happens on a real rink first
Repeats here not, for fate
Promises that, as true as bubbles burst,
The magic will dissipate.

The cat had done it. He had jumped onto the ice at the rink, and now onto the toy hockey game.

The magic was gone, and deep within him, Pie knew he was glad.

How many of these Matt Christopher sports classics have you read?

❑ Baseball Flyhawk
❑ Baseball Pals
❑ The Basket Counts
❑ Catch That Pass!
❑ Catcher with a Glass Arm
❑ Challenge at Second Base
❑ The Comeback Challenge
❑ The Counterfeit Tackle
❑ The Diamond Champs
❑ Dirt Bike Racer
❑ Dirt Bike Runaway
❑ Face-Off
❑ Football Fugitive
❑ The Fox Steals Home
❑ The Great
  Quarterback Switch
❑ Hard Drive to Short
❑ The Hockey Machine
❑ Ice Magic
❑ Johnny Long Legs
❑ The Kid Who Only
  Hit Homers
❑ Little Lefty
❑ Long Shot for Paul
❑ Long Stretch at First Base

❑ Look Who's Playing
  First Base
❑ Miracle at the Plate
❑ No Arm in Left Field
❑ Pressure Play
❑ Red-Hot Hightops
❑ Return of the
  Home Run Kid
❑ Run, Billy, Run
❑ Shoot for the Hoop
❑ Shortstop from Tokyo
❑ Skateboard Tough
❑ Soccer Halfback
❑ The Submarine Pitch
❑ Supercharged Infield
❑ Tackle Without a Team
❑ Tight End
❑ Too Hot to Handle
❑ Top Wing
❑ Touchdown for Tommy
❑ Tough to Tackle
❑ Undercover Tailback
❑ Wingman on Ice
❑ The Year Mom Won
  the Pennant

All available in paperback from Little, Brown and Company